HUNTED

Everyday Heroes Series Book One

Margaret Daley

Hunted

Copyright © 2018 by Margaret Daley

Dedication

To ordinary men
who do extraordinary deeds

ONE

Luke Michaels lay in his sleeping bag, hovering between consciousness and a dream state. A low growl yanked him wide awake. He sat straight up, still in a cocoon of warmth. Another deep rumble from Shep alerted Luke to possible danger. His German shepherd was nearby. He freed himself from his confines and scrambled to his feet.

Fearing a bear, Luke grabbed his rifle and hurried from his tent in the hills along the Kentucky River. He searched for his dog in the surrounding woods and spied him standing on a boulder overlooking the water. Tense. Alert.

In the early dawn, Luke scanned the terrain as he made his way to Shep. So focused on something in the distance, his dog didn't even acknowledge Luke's presence. He knelt next to his black and brown German shepherd and looked in the direction his dog stared.

What Luke saw chilled him in the warmth of a summer morning—a woman struggled to free herself from two men on the bridge. One guy slammed a fist into her jaw, and she went limp.

"Stay."

Barefooted, Luke plowed into the dense brush along the river, moving as fast as he could toward the trio a couple hundred yards away. Something sharp pierced the sole of his foot. He couldn't stop to see what. He kept going. His gaze shifted from the terrain to the two thugs hoisting her over the side.

Chains bound her.

Heart pounding, he stopped and raised his rifle, but before he could get off a shot, the assailants let her go. Too late.

She splashed into the water and sank

below.

Quickly, the two men disappeared from the side of the bridge. Clutching his rifle, Luke kept an eye on where she went into the river and raced as fast as he could nearer the location. He stopped on the bank closest to the area where she went under, laid his rifle down, and waded out into the cool water. He swam in the direction he thought she'd be, hoping she was still alive. The chains must have taken her to the bottom of the river. The very thought spurred him faster until he reached the spot. He dove down. The murky river limited his vision. He searched, sweeping his arms in front of him.

He didn't want to add her death to the others he hadn't been able to save. He surfaced, drew in a deep breath, then went back down. His lungs hurt. Would she even be alive if he found her?

He turned to swim up for another fortifying gulp of air when his foot brushed against something. He twisted back and felt around the muddy river. His hand encountered an arm. He couldn't waste any time bringing her to the surface.

Lungs burning, he clasped her under the arms and shot upward, her chain-clad body slowing his ascent. But he poured all his energy into kicking his legs. Finally, he broke through the surface, gulping in precious breaths while keeping her head above the water, pressing it against his as he swam for the shore a hundred feet away. He couldn't help her until he got her on land.

He dragged her out of the river and placed her on the ground. Thick chains bound her from her chest to below her knees. After he shoved them down her torso as much as he could, he immediately began chest compressions. He glanced at her beautiful face framed by shoulder length dark blonde hair.

"Live!"

She stirred, coughing and turning her head as water flowed from her mouth. Luke supported her upper body as she continued to clear her lungs. His gaze traveled down her body to assess for injuries. It was hard to tell with the shackles restraining arm and leg movement, but he didn't see any blood, except her lips where one of the men had struck her.

Finally, the woman stopped coughing and sank against his embrace, her eyelids fluttering. He pressed two fingers against her neck. Her racing pulse didn't surprise him after what she'd gone through.

"I'm Luke Michaels. Do you hurt anywhere?"

She opened her eyes, and for a few seconds, their crystalline blue color trapped him in a stare.

"No." She tried to sit up but collapsed back against him. "Yes." She drew in a breath then coughed again. "Hurt—all over."

He placed her gently on the ground. "Let me see if I can get these chains off you."

"Thanks," she murmured in a weak, raspy voice.

He tugged on the restraints, but the two padlocks holding the manacles around her remained tightly closed. "I need to take you back to my tent. I might be able to pick the locks." He looked up at the bridge—no sight of the two men. "Besides, I don't think this is a safe place to stay."

She rolled her head to the side to glance toward the bridge. "What happened?"

"Two men threw you off the bridge."

"Why?"

"You don't know?"

"No...I don't." She closed her eyes.

For a few seconds, he thought she'd passed out, but when she fixed her gaze on his face, he released a long sigh. "What do you remember?"

"Waking up—in the trunk of a car." She paused, her chest rising and falling rapidly as she sucked in shallow breaths. Panic took over her expression. Her eyes grew huge and flitted from one area to another.

Luke leaned into her line of vision. "Let's get you out of here. You're safe now." After slinging his rifle across his back, he worked his arms under her body then struggled to his feet, which painfully reminded him he'd stepped on something earlier. "My camp isn't too far from here."

While the lady rested her head against his shoulder, he retraced his path, limping the whole way back to Shep. His dog had stayed where he'd told him. Stopping near his German shepherd, Luke looked him in the eye. "Good boy. Alert."

The woman stared up at Luke. "Alert? You think those men will come here?" She tensed, fear invading her features.

"Alert is one of Shep's commands to stand guard. We're a team. We do a lot of search and rescue."

Her brows knitted together. "You were looking for me?"

"No. I like to go camping when I can get away. I was asleep when Shep alerted me that something was happening on the bridge." Luke ducked through the opening in the tent and laid her on his sleeping bag. "What's your name?"

He moved to his backpack and rummaged through it until he found his Swiss Army knife. While he went to work on the first padlock, she remained silent. After opening the lock and removing part of her chains, he glanced up to find her eyes clouded, her eyebrows scrunched. "Do you know who you are?"

"Sure," she said slowly. "I'm..." Her gaze slid away from his face.

He'd once rescued a couple of people who didn't remember anything about what had happened to them. Was she traumatized so much by what had occurred that she didn't even recall her name? After what he saw, it wouldn't surprise him if she had. He continued to work, turning his attention to the second lock. She would be sore and bruised from the shackles.

As he released the last restraints from around her, she murmured, "Megan Witherspoon. All I remember is two guys dragging me out of a trunk to the side of the bridge."

"So, you have no idea how you got into the trunk?"

Megan shook her head.

"Do you know the two men?"

"I don't think so. I only remember seeing one of them. The other was behind me."

"What did he look like?"

"He's tall and husky. Like a body builder." Kneading the back of her neck, she stared at a spot on the tent above her. "Short dark hair—no, not short but pulled back." She looked at Luke. "I think it's long, but I'm not sure. And his eyes were so dark I thought they were black."

"Where do you live?" he asked as Megan, clad in wet jeans and a hot pink T-shirt, stretched her arms and legs as though making sure they worked before she struggled to sit up. He immediately assisted her.

"Sweetwater City."

"That's twenty miles from here. Is that where they grabbed you?" Luke reached for his duffel bag and pulled it toward him.

"I—I think so." Another series of coughs racked her body, her eyes watering from the exertion.

"When that guy hit you, he cut your lip." He picked up a cloth and pressed it against her wound.

"Thanks." She took the towel and held it against her mouth.

"You need to report this to the police."

"No!" She let her hand drop away from her face. "I don't know why someone tried to kill me. All I can remember is leaving my house to run errands." Her voice quavered. "After that, nothing—until I woke up in the trunk." Frustration dominated her expression as she massaged her temples.

Why would that keep her from reporting her abduction to the authorities? "But surely the police—"

"No. Those men think they killed me. How can I protect myself if I suddenly turn up alive, especially when I'm not sure what happened or what one of them looks like?" Shivering, Megan hugged her arms.

"Nothing needs to be decided right now. You're soaking wet. I have a pair of sweat pants and a T-shirt you can put on."

"That sounds wonderful." When she smiled, her blue eyes lit as though the sun shone through them.

He rummaged through his backpack, pulling out each article of clothing. "Not quite your size but dry."

"I'll make it work." Her gaze fixed on his left foot. "You're bleeding." She gestured toward the cut.

He turned to the duffel bag and withdrew his first aid kit. "This is what happens when you run through the woods barefooted. It's nothing."

"It doesn't look like nothing to me. I can take care of it."

He started to tell her not to worry, but the concern on her face warmed his heart.

"It's the least I can do for you."

"I appreciate it." He handed her the kit and sat so his left foot was near her.

She laid his foot on her thigh then went to work, cleaning the injury then wrapping it in gauze. "You should get a tetanus shot and possibly have stitches."

"I had a tetanus shot earlier this year." Her gentle touch soothed the throbbing pain. "It looks like you've done this many times."

"I've worked with children. There. I'm done."

He started to say more, but fear and weariness carved deep lines into her face. After putting the first aid kit away, he put on his shoes and socks then stood, smiling.

"Thanks." He headed for the tent opening. "While you change, I'll make breakfast and a pot of coffee. Come out when you're ready."

As Luke left Megan, one question came to the foreground. She couldn't have been running errands today because it was six o'clock in the morning. So, when was she kidnapped? His mind raced with hundreds of scenarios that could have landed her in this predicament. If only she remembered where she'd been, when she was there, and what made two men abduct her. The not knowing could definitely get her killed.

* * *

Dressed in dry clothes, Megan glanced down at her attire of baggy, twice-her-size sweatpants while the T-shirt fell just above her knees. A chuckle escaped until she remembered being carried to the side of the bridge, chains encasing her. All she could do was buck and twist as she fought to escape her frightening fate. What happened to her to put her in that situation?

Why can't I remember?

A wave of tremors swamped her. She sank to the ground and wrapped her arms around her torso as she shook. She couldn't let fear keep her from recalling the details that led to those kidnappers throwing her off the bridge. If she couldn't figure that out, she would never be safe. And she had to be. School was starting in almost two weeks. She could never put her elementary students in danger.

What errands was I running?

That has to be the key.

She drew her legs up to her chest and clasped them, resting her head in the crook between her knees. But she couldn't even picture getting up this morning.

She straightened. Duh! She couldn't be running errands this early, which meant she was kidnapped before today. So, it wasn't just a few hours she couldn't remember but possibly days.

How long have I been gone from my house?

"Megan, are you all right?" Luke asked

from the other side of the canvas opening.

His deep, husky voice sent a shiver of reassurance through her that she was safe for the time being. But then she really didn't know her rescuer other than his name. Luke Michaels.

Why did that name sound familiar?

Did he live in Sweetwater City? He didn't say he did.

"Megan?"

"I'm fine," she finally answered in a scratchy voice, her throat sore. She reached for her still-wet belt and strapped it around the top of the sweat pants. Coughing, she pushed to her feet, moved the flap to the side, and ducked out of the tent. "Sorry. I was trying to figure out how I was going to keep these pants up. Thankfully I recalled my belt."

He smiled, a dimple appearing in each cheek. His gray eyes shone like polished silver. "Do you want coffee?"

"Yes." She hoped the hot brew would warm her insides and soothe her throat. Despite the temperature hovering around seventy, she couldn't rid her body of a deep chill.

He covered the distance to the cooking stove, stooped and filled two cups, then handed her one. "Take a seat." He swept an arm toward a small table with two chairs. "I went back to my SUV and got an extra chair and a few more dishes."

As she sat, she glanced around at his equipment and supplies. "Do you go camping a lot?"

"Yes." He placed his coffee on the table then took two paper plates and dished up the scrambled eggs and bacon. When he brought them to the table, he set one in front of her. "Shep and I are often involved in search and rescues in this area but also around the country, so I have to be prepared for anything. I keep my SUV stocked with a lot of emergency supplies. Sometimes, I don't have much time to pack because I need to get to the rescue spot quickly." He eased into the chair across from her. His brown dog with large patches of black moved to lie next to him.

"So, you live in this area?"

"Yes, on a horse farm between

Lexington and Sweetwater City."

She sipped her coffee, relishing the warmth. "Well, I'm glad you were here today. I owe you my life. Thank you."

His short brown hair was nearly dry after his plunge into the Kentucky River. "If Shep hadn't growled, I wouldn't have known about you." He reached down and rubbed his dog.

"May I pet him?"

"Sure. He loves people."

Megan knelt next to Shep and held her hand out for him to smell. He licked her fingers. She laughed and stroked his back. "Good boy. I hear you're my hero. Thanks."

Shep rolled over and exposed his belly.

Megan shifted her attention to that area.

"He likes you. I've never seen him do that with others."

"I'm glad. He's a beauty." She returned to her scrambled eggs. "When I was a little girl, I had a German shepherd. Her name was Lady although she rarely acted like one. She'd get into all kind of messes. Once she ate part of a white cake with a lot of icing for my birthday that was on the counter in the kitchen. She left me half. I didn't eat it, but I was tempted. I love cake, especially with thick icing."

Luke chuckled. "Wise decision."

"I'm an animal lover. What's the name of your horse farm?"

"Riverdale Farm." He finished a piece of bacon then turned his attention to his eggs.

So that was why she knew his name. Every year she watched the Kentucky Derby. He had two winners in the past five or six years. "You own Lightning Bolt?"

"Yes. I put him out to stud this year."

"It's rare for a horse to be a Triple Crown Winner. I was cheering him on. Is he stabled at Riverdale?"

"Yes. And spoiled rotten. Do you want anything else to eat?" he asked as she finished the last bite of her breakfast.

"No, but it was delicious. I usually don't eat bacon, but it was great. I guess when you come close to death you perceive things differently." *I know I have You to thank, Lord. You sent someone to rescue me. Now I need help figuring out what's going on*.

"Have you thought about what you're going to do next?"

She wanted to say hide, but where would she be safe? "Any suggestions besides going to the police in Sweetwater City?"

He opened his mouth to answer, but before he could, Shep jumped to his feet, a low growl emitting from between his bared teeth.

TWO

Luke quickly grabbed his rifle and put himself between Megan and the area where Shep centered his attention. Through the foliage, he spied the culprit. "It's a medium-sized black bear. He must have gotten a whiff of the bacon."

Megan stood up. "What should I do?"

"At the moment, nothing. My car is about five hundred yards away. Too far to make a dash for it. Shep, speak."

His dog's fierce snarl turned to barking.

"He isn't going to fight the bear, is he?" Megan's voice sounded faint over the loud noise coming from his German shepherd.

"No. Unless I give him the command,

Shep will stay put." A minute later, the bear ambled back into the denser vegetation. Shep continued to yelp and growl until Luke said, "Shep, stop."

Silence reigned almost instantly.

"I have a dog. She isn't nearly trained as well as Shep. Oh, no!"

Luke spun around and faced Megan whose hand covered her mouth, her eyes round. "What's wrong?"

"I don't know how long I've been gone. Lady's been alone—possibly for days. What day is it?"

"Friday."

Her tensed shoulders sagged. "Good. That means I've only been gone a day."

"You've remembered more of what happened?"

The words had just come out of her mouth. Then she recalled why. "Not much but Thursday was the day I was going to run errands. I need to get home. She's probably worried where I am."

"I agree we should leave, but I still think you need to go to the police first. I know the police chief in Sweetwater City."

20

She shook her head. "First, I want to get Lady. I know I'm in danger if the two kidnappers discover I'm alive, but my poodle is like a member of my family."

"Lady is a poodle? This isn't the dog you talked about earlier?"

"No. I named my poodle after my German shepherd I had years ago."

"I'll pack up the car before the bear gets the idea to return. We'll go by your house and pick up Lady and whatever else you'll need for the next week or so. It's probably not a good idea for you to stay at your place until we figure out what's going on." *We* had slipped out before he realized it. He'd saved her, and he had no intention of those two thugs finding her and completing the job.

"I'm still not sure about going to the police station."

"Why?"

"I don't know, but every time you mention the police, my stomach tightens."

"I've worked closely with Chief Franklin several times on search and rescues." Could one of his officers be involved in what happened to Megan? He didn't want to believe that. Joe Franklin was dedicated to his job to the point he went above and beyond in every situation Luke had dealt with him. "How about I have the police chief meet us somewhere privately? He could search quietly to see where your car was left. That might help you remember what happened."

"That would probably be okay. What can I do to help you pack your car?" She gestured toward the camping equipment around her. Something was wrong. She examined her right hand.

"Is something wrong?"

"I lost my ring." She stared at her middle finger. "I always wear it." Glancing in the direction of the river, she blinked the tears forming from her eyes. "I must have lost it in the water. I always take it off when I go swimming."

"I didn't notice one when I was carrying you."

"It was my mother's."

"Sit. It won't take me long to dismantle the tent and pack up everything."

"But I can help—"

"Megan, you went through a traumatic experience an hour ago. Rest when you can." The only reason he would take her to her house was the fact the bad guys thought they had killed her. They wouldn't be looking for her. He would call Chief Franklin after that. Until she remembered what had happened over the past twenty-four hours, she wouldn't be safe.

She took her cup to the stove and poured more coffee into it. Then she sat in her camping chair. Color returned to her face, but worry was still visible in her eyes. He was concerned for her, too. Sweetwater City was a quiet town of forty thousand. Several times the police chief had mentioned the low crime rate, so what had Megan stumbled into?

Ten minutes later, he had all his belongings packed. He slung his backpack over his shoulders then picked up the tent. "I won't be gone long." He started in the direction of his car.

"Wait. What can I carry? I'll follow you."

He stopped and glanced back at her.

"Shep, stay. Guard. I'll be back in a few minutes, Megan."

Despite the cut on the bottom of his foot hurting, he jogged down the narrow path to his SUV. Shep would protect her, but Luke didn't want to be gone long. As he quickly loaded his car and returned to the camp, he made a decision he hoped Megan would accept. He took his job as a rescuer seriously. He would never let another person down again. The one time he failed his wife, she'd died because he couldn't reach her in time. Her family didn't blame him, but he did.

As he emerged into the small clearing, Megan's gaze was trained on Shep nearby. "I think we—"

She gasped as she twisted toward him. "Shep didn't indicate you were coming. How could he tell it was you?"

"My scent. We're a team. Have been for five years. Are you ready to leave?"

She nodded. "What do you want me to take?"

"What you're sitting on. I can get the rest."

She opened her mouth to say something. Instead, she snapped it closed and folded up her chair while he picked up the duffel bag holding the stove, the cooking dishes, and the utensils. After he hefted the box of food, he headed toward his chair.

Megan moved in his path and blocked him, her chin tilted up. "I can manage both yours and mine."

"Okay." Chuckling, he went around her and led the way to the SUV with Megan and Shep following.

After he loaded the rest of the car, he put Shep into his kennel tied down in the cargo area. Megan slipped into the passenger seat, a long sigh escaping her lips as he slammed the rear door closed.

"I don't remember much of the past twenty-four hours except getting into my car and backing out of my driveway, but I'm exhausted," she said as he climbed into the driver's seat. "I feel like I've run a marathon in record time."

"Near death situations can do that to you." Luke started the engine then pulled out onto the dirt road. "What kind of job do you have? Maybe your errands had something to do with that."

"I'm an elementary teacher at the main school campus for Sweetwater City where my building is as well as a middle and high school one and the administration building. I've been there several times this summer, but I can't remember going there yesterday or when I was taken."

"Do you live alone?"

"Yes, in my family home. It's just Lady and me since my mother died last year."

"Would there be anyone who would miss you if you were gone for any length of time?" Luke turned onto the two-lane highway leading to her town.

"I had a sister who died as a child, and my father left years ago. He cut off all ties with us. I have no close relatives."

"Friends? People you work with?"

"Possibly my neighbors, like Louise next door. She seems to know everything on the block. Another is a teacher I work with. Sally might notice if I was unexpectedly gone for several days, but I doubt she would if it was only one. Another good friend I talk with a lot is in Europe with her husband."

"And you're sure you were running errands yesterday?"

"I think so, but truthfully, when I'm on vacation, the days run together for me. Now if it was during the school year, I would know exactly. I have a set routine but purposefully avoid one when I'm not teaching. That's the rebel in me." Megan sent him a smile and relaxed back against the headrest.

"I know what you mean. When I retired from my job on Wall Street, it was a cultural shock to my system. Life on a horse farm and work in the financial district are totally different."

"You're retired? You look about thirty."

He chuckled. "I'm thirty-seven, and I've been retired from Wall Street since I was thirty-three." Even before his wife had died and everything fell apart, consuming wealth had dominated too much of his life.

"What made you buy a horse farm?"

"I didn't. It's been in my family for

decades, handed down from one generation to the next. My parents retired to Florida and turned it over to my sister and me. We run it together. But enough about me. What made you become a teacher?"

"A lot of teachers in my family. My mother loved being one. But the real reason is that I enjoy working with children and helping them navigate through this world."

He and his wife, Rochelle, had wanted kids, but their busy lives had forced them to postpone the wish until "life settled down," which never seemed to happen. He shook the memory from his mind. He needed to remain focused on Megan. She was in trouble.

As he neared the outskirts of Sweetwater City, Megan's demeanor changed. For a while when they talked about their work, she had relaxed. Now she sat up straight, her shoulders tensed, her cheeks pale. She chewed on the side of her bottom lip that hadn't gotten cut and clenched her hands in her lap.

He slanted her a glance. "You'll be

okay. I'll be there with you."

* * *

Although Luke's presence reassured her that she wouldn't be alone, Megan couldn't stamp down the fear oozing through her body. She remembered the moment when she realized the two kidnappers were going to throw her off that high bridge. No matter what she did, she wasn't able to fight them, not with her legs and arms shackled to her sides. The heavy chains had weighed her down, and she had plunged to the bottom of the river to die. And she couldn't even recall why.

That was when she'd twisted and done whatever she could while she called out to the Lord. The captor she'd gotten a look at had laughed and punched her. She touched the sore left side of her face and wondered if she would have a bruise.

But she was here now. God sent her a rescuer. Maybe the two men didn't have a reason to abduct her other than to terrorize her. There were people like that in the world. They could have been driving through the town, spotted her, and taken her on impulse. By now, they might be out of the state. Maybe Luke was right, and she should report it to the police. But the thought churned her stomach.

She ignored that reaction. "You're right about reporting it to the police. I was letting fear take over." Megan flexed her fingers and shook them to release the tension. Luke would be with her. She would be all right.

"Perfectly understandable. We'll go to your house first, so you can get your dog. I'll call Chief Franklin to come over then."

She smiled. "That sounds good, especially the part about making sure Lady is all right."

"That's how I would feel concerning Shep. How old is Lady?"

"Three. And she thinks she runs the house. She's very smart. She drove me crazy because she wanted to go outside all the time. I finally put in a doggie door. She's small so I was able to get one that a person couldn't crawl through."

"Did you ever take her to an obedience school?"

Megan laughed. "Yes, and she failed the course. That was when she was around a year old. Lady is stubborn about a couple of things, but otherwise she's been a good dog. She loves people."

"I'll need directions to your place."

"Sure. Stay on this road for three stoplights and then turn left onto Pine. Go two miles and take a right onto Lakeshore Drive. My house is the third on the left." She couldn't wait until she held Lady. Her dog always knew when something was wrong and had a way of centering Megan so she could move forward. "Although I live on Lakeshore Drive, you have to go almost two more miles before you come to the small lake. If I want to jog around it, I have to drive my car to the park near it and start from there."

"Do you jog a lot?" Luke headed down Pine.

"About once a year, when we jog around the lake to raise money for the school where I teach." The prospects of seeing the haven she'd lived in all her life lent lightness to her reply. "In my defense, I do exercise, but I prefer biking."

When Luke turned onto Lakeshore Drive, Megan shifted her attention in the direction of her house as she sat forward filled with eagerness.

She gasped at the burnt remnants of what used to be her home.

THREE

Stunned, Luke gripped his steering wheel and stared at the destroyed structure with the brick fireplace still standing tall while the walls were burned in many places to the foundation.

Megan put her hand on the handle and pushed the door open.

"Don't!"

She glanced over her shoulder at Luke, devastation carved into her facial features from her furrowed brow to the anguish in her eyes. "I have to find Lady. She can't be—" Her words came to a halt as tears ran down her cheeks.

"It's too dangerous. I'll go look for

Lady. Stay in the car where no one can see you. My windows are dark, but I'd get down on the floor to be on the safe side."

After pushing the seat as far back as she could, Megan scrunched down on the floorboard in front of it. "She's a white miniature poodle. Why would someone burn my home down?"

"It looks like it was done yesterday. The yellow tape is up, and I don't see any smoke coming from the rubble." He climbed from his vehicle. "I'm locking the doors. If someone tries to get in, honk. I'm letting Shep out in the back. If a person comes near, he'll bark."

At the rear of his SUV, Luke opened Shep's kennel. His German shepherd jumped out, so he could hop into the front. After giving his dog the command to guard, Luke strode with a slight limp toward the ruins, wanting to find out how the fire started and when. He could call Chief Franklin, but he wasn't sure bringing attention to the fact Megan was with him would be the right thing to do. There were so many unanswered questions about what was going on, especially in light of her house being burned down. And he now couldn't totally dismiss Megan's initial reaction of being frightened when he mentioned the police. His gut instinct demanded he wait until he could take Megan somewhere safe.

As Luke rounded the side of the house, he noticed an older woman in her backyard leaning against the fence. He covered the distance to her. "I'm Luke, a friend of Megan's from out of town."

She cupped her ear. "I'm a little hard of hearing. What's your name?"

Luke repeated in a loud voice what he'd told her a moment ago. "I'm shocked to see her place is gone. What happened here?"

"I'm Louise. I can't believe she's dead."

"Dead? I didn't see anything in the news about her dying."

Megan's next-door neighbor shook her head. "It was awful. I was fixin' to go to bed when I saw her house engulfed in flames." She pointed at a side window on her place. "I called the fire department, but

they were already on the way. Another neighbor or Megan must have notified them, too."

Worried about Megan in his car by herself, Luke stamped down his impatience and asked, "What makes you think Megan's dead?"

The gray-haired woman's eyes grew saucer wide. "Because the firefighters found a dead body in there." She waved her hand toward the destruction. "Near the front door. Megan had been so close to saving herself."

"How about Lady? Did they find her?"

"No." Tears glistened in her eyes. "Such a sweet dog. They still might, though. There was a lot of smoldering debris. It's just now cooling down. The police and firefighters couldn't really search through the rubble. They'll be here in an hour or two. I'm making sure no one disturbs the place. When I saw Chief Franklin earlier this morning, I told him I would. I look after my neighbors."

"Where's the dead body now?"

"The firefighters removed it, and the

police took it away. Charred beyond recognition. Such a beautiful woman. So sad."

"How do they know it was Megan?"

"There was a ring on her hand that I recognized was hers. It was her mother's. When she died last year, Megan started wearing it to keep a part of her mom close to her."

Luke knew it would take more than that to identify the body as Megan's. But letting people think it was Megan in her house might give them time to figure out what was going on. "Do you mind if I look around? Maybe Lady got out of the home in time. Megan told me she'd had a doggie door installed."

Louise cocked her head. "You know you're right. I didn't think about that. Not surprised I didn't. I was so upset and up most of the night because of the fire."

"I know Megan would want me to take Lady and care for her."

"How sweet. I'd take her except that I have two cats that don't care for any dog, especially Lady."

"I understand." Luke started for the fenced backyard. If Lady made it outside in time, she would probably be hiding somewhere there if she didn't make a getaway while the gate was open.

He stood a few feet from the patio. "Lady," he called several times while he visually swept the area. There was only one place where it would be good for Lady to hide. He marched across the grass to the rear along the chain-link fence where three large, lush bushes grew. After kneeling on the ground, he leaned down and spied a fluff of white fur in the midst of the green foliage.

Luke grabbed a doggie treat from his pocket that he carried for Shep and slid his hand under the brush. "Lady, it's yours." He held it up and shook it then placed it back on the dirt. When the poodle crawled forward, he left his hand nearby. As Lady enjoyed the beef delight, he stroked her. She finished, and he added, "Want another, Lady?" He laid it on the grass in front of him. "Come and get it."

Slowly the poodle inched closer. Black

streaks covered her white fur on the sides. Had she tried to go back inside after everyone left? He gently lifted her front paw and saw the reddened pad. He scooped up the fluffy ball into his arms. The dog's body shook against him. "You're safe, Lady." Then he inspected the rest of her feet. Relieved she wasn't injured badly and only on one paw, he cradled her and rose.

Before heading to his SUV, he continued his trek around the house, checking the debris as he made his way to his car. He knocked on the front passenger side window to alert Megan to his presence. She stared up at him with wide eyes, but when she saw him and then Lady, a smile erased all fear from her expression.

He pressed his key fob, unlocking his vehicle, and transferred the poodle to Megan, making sure he didn't open the door too wide. Louise watched from where he'd left her earlier. "I have salve that I can put on her right front paw that's red. I think she tried to go into the house before it completely cooled down. I found her under the bushes at the rear of your property," he whispered, his back to her neighbor.

She hugged Lady against her while checking on her poodle's injury. "Thanks for finding her. I don't know what I would have..." she cleared her throat "...done. The best thing I did was to install that doggie door."

"Be back in a sec. Kennel, Shep," he said to his dog, whose head was resting on Megan's shoulder while he watched Lady. When Luke arrived at the rear door, Shep hopped over the backseat and went into his kennel. "Good boy." He offered him a treat then rummaged through his duffel bag for his well-stocked medical supplies he always took when he went to a search and rescue or on a camping trip.

He sat behind the steering wheel and passed the ointment to Megan. "It doesn't look too bad."

She applied the burn balm. "She's a quick learner. That's why I was surprised she didn't do well in obedience class."

"Maybe you should try again. Age can bring wisdom." Luke glimpsed toward where the neighbor had been and noticed Louise crossing Megan's yard, heading for him.

She laughed. "For who? Me or Lady?"

He started the car and quickly pulled away from the curb. Good thing Megan was still down. For the time being, he was glad Louise and others thought Megan was the victim found in her house. "Of course, I meant Lady."

"Are you still going to see the police chief?"

"I have something I need to tell you first."

* * *

In the right-side mirror, Megan caught sight of Louise standing near the curb, watching Luke drive away from Megan's house. "Did you talk with my neighbor?"

"Yes."

"When did the fire start?" After settling in the passenger seat, she placed Lady in her lap and stroked her.

"Around the time Louise went to bed."

"She usually retires early between eight and nine." Her covered walkway and detached garage had minimal damage. Her car could be inside. She pressed her fingertips against her temple and massaged it as though that action would magically return her memory to what had happened to her when she ran her errands.

"So right after dark. That makes sense. My theory is one or both of the men came to your house and torched it, but not before they left a body inside to burn."

She whipped her head around to look at Luke. A dead body in her house? The thought heightened her fear. "What body? Why would they do that?"

"The police think it's you. According to your neighbor, the body was badly burned, which makes it hard to identify. Maybe your abductors wanted it to appear as though you were in the house."

"Why do the police think it's me?"

"The woman was wearing your mother's ring you wear all the time."

Megan stared at her right hand where the ring usually was. "So, I didn't lose it in the river. The kidnappers took it." *What's going on? What did I see?* "If anyone knows what's happening, it would be Louise. I love her, but she's a busybody." Her heartbeat accelerated, its pounding hammering against her skull.

"Good thing we got away before she saw you in my car."

"Yeah. I don't want her to get hurt. She's been a good neighbor for years. I need to warn her."

"I think you need to get out of town. Contacting Louise could put her in danger, especially if she starts asking questions and the wrong person hears. My horse farm is only forty-five minutes away. We need to think carefully about our next move."

"We? Our?" She liked the sound of those words. She didn't feel so alone, but he'd already put himself in danger by rescuing her. "What about the police chief? Aren't you going to call him and meet with him?"

"I'm having second thoughts until we can figure out what's going on. Whoever is behind this won't hesitate to kill. Chief

Franklin is someone I've worked with on several rescues but not a close friend. He seems trustworthy, but if I'm wrong, the price is too high."

Was she being naïve to trust Luke Michaels? She knew of him, and what she'd heard and read about him had been positive, but the only one she could trust totally was the Lord. *What do I do, God?*

"You'll be safe at my farm. My sister stays in the main house. My housekeeper and farm manager as well as several hands live in other buildings there, and because of the expensive studs I have, my security is good. But even better, we didn't know each other until this morning. I only told Louise my first name. No one will know you're at my house. You can stay there under an assumed name."

"You sound like you're familiar with security measures. About all I've ever done is lock my doors. I've lived in Sweetwater City all my life and know a lot of the people. The town has grown since I was a child, but it still feels like a small town to me."

"What do you want me to do? Call the police chief, take you to my farm, or something else? I'll do what you want."

Her options were limited. She could go to a motel in Sweetwater City or somewhere like Lexington. She could stay with a friend or her cousin who lived in Louisville. Or go with Luke and try to figure out what was going on. By herself, she had no idea where to start. The only books she read were romances. No mysteries or suspense stories except when she was a child and devoured the Nancy Drew series.

Megan slanted a look toward Luke as he drove. His strong profile put her at ease. "At least for tonight, I'll stay at your farm and try to find out about the fire at my house. It might be on the news tonight." Her stomach gurgled.

"Hungry?" he asked as he left the city limits.

"Yes. It seems that fighting for your life zaps your energy."

"There's a country café between here and my place. We can stop there. They have sandwiches we can take with us. I don't think you should go inside. Someone might remember seeing you when the story breaks about the fire."

She gestured at his clothes she was wearing. "And I'm sure I would draw attention if I went inside."

His smile dimpled his cheeks. "Good point. They have great chicken salad or roast beef sandwiches."

"I'll take chicken salad. May I turn on the Sweetwater City radio station? At the top of the hour, they have news and often cover local events. Maybe I'll get more information about what's going on."

"Sure."

While Megan changed the channel, Luke increased his speed on the highway. When a current popular song played, the reception clear, she reclined back, trying to relax as much as possible. She slid her eyes closed except for a slit. She studied her rescuer, his attention on the road as he drove sixty-five miles per hour. His day-old beard highlighted his rugged features. His persona shouted his self-confidence, but while they had talked, there had been a glimpse of vulnerability in his gray eyes when he'd mentioned retiring from Wall Street. What was the story behind him leaving New York City and returning to his family farm?

The mention of her name on the radio yanked her from her musings. "If anyone knows the whereabouts of Megan Witherspoon, please contact the Sweetwater City Police Department. She's a person of interest in the house fire on Lakeshore Drive last night where one person died."

FOUR

Luke glanced at Megan, her back stiff, her mouth hanging open. He switched off the car radio and pulled onto the shoulder of the road.

Megan turned toward him, her face pale. "Didn't Louise say the police are considering that the dead person is me? Do the police really think I killed whoever was in the house and set fire to my home? What's going on?"

"Since you own the house, you would be a person of interest. Until they can identify the body, they're required to search for you. I don't think they're saying you're a killer. They may not even consider the dead person murdered, but a victim of the fire."

She dropped her head and kneaded her nape. "What happened yesterday? What have I gotten involved in? My life has always been routine and honestly dull. The most exciting thing that's occurred this past year is being named the teacher of the year at the Sweetwater City Public Schools."

"I'd say that's quite an accomplishment." He took his SUV out of *park* and returned to the highway. "I'm not going to stop for sandwiches. It's best we get to my place and see what else we can find out. I'll call Chief Franklin and ask him if he needs Shep and me to search for you. Maybe I can get some information about what's going on."

"Like where's my car? In the detached garage or somewhere else in Sweetwater?"

"That's a good idea."

As he drove toward his farm, Megan settled back against the seat and closed her eyes. Her physical and emotional trauma would catch up with her soon. Adrenaline would only work for so long.

Whatever was going on involved more people than the two thugs and Megan. Who was the dead person in her house? Had the body been there before Megan's home was set on fire? How could he help her remember how she ended up on the bridge? The past few years, he'd worked with a lot of law enforcement officers, but piecing a case together wasn't his area of expertise.

He tried calling his younger sister, Liliana, but her phone went to voicemail. He wished she would keep her cell turned on all the time, especially during the workweek. Usually that meant she was riding her mare. He hadn't wanted to surprise her with his guest.

When he saw the gates to Riverdale Farm twenty-five minutes later, he relaxed his tight grip on the steering wheel and released a long breath. He reached toward the passenger side for the gate opener attached to the backside of the visor.

Megan shot up and looked out the windshield, her hand on her chest over her heart. "You're home?"

"Yes. Welcome to Riverdale Farm." He pressed the button and the black wrought-iron gates swung open.

"I must have fallen asleep. I didn't think I could." Megan panned the fields as they drove by. "I'm glad we're here. The first thing I want to do is wash my clothes. I appreciate the use of yours, but I can only imagine how ridiculous I look."

He assessed her with a sweep of his gaze. Swathed in yards of material, she looked vulnerable, yet with all that had happened in a short time, she'd managed to keep herself together. "Not ridiculous. Miraculous that you're here."

"You were in the right place at the right time. God placed you in my path."

Then why didn't God help him save his wife? "I'm not so sure He did that." Luke pulled up to his white antebellum home with its four large columns in front.

"I am. I have a purpose that He still needs me to do."

The confident expression on her face stunned him. She really believed that. There had been a time when he'd thought that.

"Things happen for a reason. Sometimes we never will know why, but there's a plan for you if you choose to follow it."

He harrumphed. "There was a time I would have agreed." He opened his SUV door. "Let's go inside. Since it's near lunch, my sister should be around."

Megan climbed down with Lady in her arms.

Luke let Shep out of his kennel. His German shepherd started for the pair.

"Heel," Luke commanded.

His dog turned around and came back to Luke's side and walked with him as he joined Megan and her dog.

Lady yelped, trying to wiggle from Megan's arms. She held her more firmly, and her poodle began growling instead of barking. "She thinks she's protecting me. She can get fierce."

"Thankfully, Shep can be patient. When we get inside, we'll let them get acquainted with each other." Luke started for the verandah, keeping his dog on the opposite side from Megan.

His sister swung the front door open. "I thought you were staying for two days." Her gaze skipped to Megan then back to him.

"My plans changed. Liliana, this is Megan Witherspoon."

Megan smiled. "Nice to meet you. Don't pay attention to Lady. She'll settle down. She's a little distraught. My house burned down with her inside."

"It burned down! Oh, I'm so sorry. Where do you live?"

"Sweetwater City." Lady shifted between barking and growling. "Maybe she's more upset than a little." Megan's cheeks reddened.

Liliana chuckled. "I love poodles. I used to have one. I know how strong-minded they can be. C'mon inside where it's cooler, and you can tell me how you two know each other." She winked at him.

Luke followed his sister and Megan into the large foyer. "Let's see if we can introduce Lady and Shep first. Put her down on the floor but still have a hold on her. Shep, stay."

Megan squatted and set Lady on the marble floor. "What's next?"

"I'm going to bring Shep slowly closer," he said over Lady's barking.

As the German shepherd neared the poodle, she stopped yelping and kept her attention on the large dog. Lady occasionally emitted a low growl.

"Release your hold and let's see what they do." Luke knelt next to his pet. "Sit."

Shep did and focused on the small white dog in front of him. He lowered his head and sniffed the air around Lady. She inched closer and smelled Shep's front paws. Shep licked the top of the poodle's head.

Luke tensed, and Megan reached for Lady. She slipped from her owner's grasp and charged Shep, slobbered on his nearest foot, then darted back to Megan. The poodle began barking again, but the tone was different, as though she was playing a game with Shep. His dog plopped down on the floor and stretched out as Lady ran circles around him.

Megan stood, chuckling. "The neighbors across the street have a black Lab, and Lady plays with her all the time. But then there's another big dog in the park she actually chases away from her."

"My poodle was called Susie, and she was black. Shep came to live here a few years ago. Susie was fifteen, and he was especially gentle with her as her health began to decline." Liliana looked around at the duffel bag and backpack that he'd brought inside. "Do you have any belongings, Megan?"

"A wet pair of jeans and a shirt that's probably dry by now." She pointed to her feet. "And these damp tennis shoes."

"Obviously there's a story behind why you're wearing Luke's clothes and yours are wet."

"I met Megan while she was drowning in the river. I saved her."

Liliana's forehead furrowed. "I have a ton of questions, but first thing you should do is change into clothes that actually fit. I think," Liliana ran her gaze down Megan's length, "I have clothes that are your size.

Why don't you come upstairs and pick out something to wear? Then I'll throw a load into the washing machine with your items. I have some sandals that should be your size. I'll wash your tennis shoes too."

Megan smiled. "That sounds wonderful. If it wasn't for my belt, I wouldn't even be able to wear these sweatpants."

Liliana mounted the first stair. "Were you there when your house caught on fire?"

"No, I wasn't there when it happened," Megan said with a touch of pain as she followed his sister up to the second floor.

"You were at the river?"

"Not exactly the river but the bridge over it."

Luke started to interrupt Liliana about discussing what happened to Megan then decided that she could determine how much she wanted his sister to know. Liliana knew how to keep a secret. He didn't want anyone else at Riverdale to know who Megan was or why she was here—not that he thought any of his employees would turn her in. But if just one of them let something slip, that could lead to the people who tried to kill her finding out where she was. He was hoping in the next day or so that Megan would start remembering what occurred yesterday. Maybe in a safe environment, her memory would return.

* * *

In the deserted, darkened corridor, Megan removed her sunglasses as she started toward her classroom. When she rounded the corner, she spotted a large man with dark hair leave the women's restroom for teachers at the far end of the hall and exit the school building through a door that remained locked during the summer. When she came to ready her class for the coming school year, the north door was the only one kept unlocked during the daytime. She neared the bathroom to enter, partially curious why that man came out of it.

Megan reached out to push the door open. Her hand shook as she touched it. She came to a halt, bringing her arm back to her side. Sweat popped out on her upper lip. She couldn't move as though frozen to the floor. Her heartbeat echoed through her head.

A yelp penetrated her mind. The pressure of tiny paws on her chest demanded her full attention, drawing her away from the looming metal restroom door.

Her eyes flew open, and she stared at a burgundy canopy above, her mind groggy as if halfway between the world of sleep and wakefulness.

Where am I?

Another bark lanced through her skull, and she rolled her head to the side.

Lady licked Megan's face then nudged her.

I'm at Luke's place. The thought calmed her racing heartbeat. Safe.

"Do you need to go outside?"

Her poodle flew off the bed and stood by the closed door, prancing side to side—a sign she couldn't wait much longer.

Megan hurried, slipping a pair of Liliana's sandals on as she covered the space between them. "Hold it."

Out in the corridor, she looked up and down the hall, confused for a few seconds which way to go. She couldn't forget the fear that had held her immobile before the restroom door. Lady ran to the left, and Megan quickly followed, rounding a corner and spying the staircase. She was glad her dog remembered the way. Luke's house was huge. As though Lady knew the home well, she charged down the steps and across the large foyer. She paced in front of the double doors that led outside.

Megan didn't have a leash with her. The thought made her hesitate letting Lady outside, but a series of yaps urged her to move faster. The second there was room, Lady bolted through the narrow opening. She found a patch of green grass near the verandah and relieved herself.

"I'm glad you got some rest," Luke said in a deep, husky voice coming from the left.

Her breath caught for a few seconds before she remembered to exhale. She turned in his direction.

"You didn't get any rest?" Luke sat in a

white wicker chair in a grouping at the far end of the verandah.

"Am I that obvious?"

"Did something happen? You were so tired when you went upstairs to take a nap, I thought you might sleep for hours."

After glancing over her shoulder to make sure Lady was still nearby, Megan moved toward him and took a seat with an end table between them. "I had a weird dream. It seemed so real."

"Maybe it was. What was it about?"

Megan told him about going to the school and seeing a man coming out of the women's restroom. "I couldn't make myself open the door. I wanted to go in, but fear paralyzed me. Then I woke up. Do you think it could have something to do with my kidnapping?"

"Did you recognize who the man was?"

She shook her head. "I didn't see his face."

"How did you know it was a man?"

"Well...I don't know. Maybe it was his build and the way he walked." She shrugged. "It was probably nothing."

"Or your subconscious is trying to tell you something, possibly about yesterday."

"And I'm blocking it?"

"Maybe. Let's see what the local news says this evening. You went through a traumatic incident, and your mind is trying to protect you by keeping you in the dark."

She smiled. "You sound like a therapist."

He scrunched his forehead, and his eyes clouded as though he was remembering something in the past. "I had one tell me that once."

"Did you eventually remember?" She wanted to ask him what happened, but she didn't want to pry.

He stared at the front yard. "Yes, when I was better able to deal with it."

The sadness in his expression made her wonder if he had really dealt with it, but it wasn't her place to ask. She wished she could help him. He'd certainly been there for her when she needed it. "But I have to remember now, or I'll never feel safe."

"You're not alone."

The intensity in his eyes gave her a

feeling of security. *Thank You, Lord, for sending him to rescue me.*

Lady's high-pitched yelps filled the air. She swiveled her attention in the direction of the sound and stood as her poodle charged Shep, who was lying on the grass.

"They're all right. I've been watching them. They're playing."

Lady jumped over Shep's back then ran around the German shepherd several times, barking the whole time as though challenging the bigger dog to get her. Instead, Shep rolled over, his tail wagging.

"He has the patience of Job." Megan took a seat again.

"Yes, and he's teaching me the importance of it."

"My students do that every year."

"What grade do you teach?"

"Third, for the last few years." She panned the landscape of gently rolling hills and pastures full of horses. "Your farm is beautiful."

"Would you like a tour?"

"Yes, but what about your employees seeing me? They might recognize me from the news?"

He frowned. "Surely we can come up with something to disguise you as a precaution."

"Great! Will I get to see Lightning Bolt?"

"I think I can manage it." Luke rose. "Let's round up the dogs then go see what Liliana has that you can use."

"I thought she was going to the stables." Megan pushed to her feet.

"That's right. She won't mind. I know just what I'm looking for." He whistled. "Come, Shep."

The German shepherd jumped up and made a beeline for Luke, and Lady followed the big dog.

Fifteen minutes later, Megan stood before a mirror in the entry hall, staring at the image of her as a light brunette with red highlights and a mop of long curls. She'd never worn a wig before. When she slipped on a pair of large, dark sunglasses, she didn't even recognize herself. She turned toward Luke. "How do I look?"

He chuckled. "That can be a loaded question for a man. The disguise is good.

Where's Lady?"

"I left her in my room. I don't have her leash, and I certainly don't want to see her challenge a horse. It might not be as accommodating as Shep."

"True. We have some temperamental Thoroughbreds. But I will say, Lightning Bolt loves Shep."

"That's because he knows how to behave. Lady doesn't."

Luke held the front door open for Megan, and she exited first. The sun, heading for the western horizon, looked as though it was floating on top of a grove of tall trees near one of the Riverdale's stables, their destination.

"We'll need to be back for the local news. I wonder if the authorities have figured out the dead body at my house isn't me. Maybe they already have, and that's why I'm a person of interest?"

"That's a possibility. I have a good friend who's part of the state police. I thought I'd call him later and see what I can find out about the case."

"What about Chief Franklin?"

"Let's see what Clay tells me. After seeing your burned down house and learning there was a dead body in it, my gut tells me to be cautious with whom we trust. Remember when I first mentioned contacting the police chief, you didn't want me to."

"But I don't know why I didn't. Maybe I was just panicking. I know who Chief Franklin is, but I don't know him other than casually. I keep trying to remember yesterday, but I get nothing—other than that dream I told you about. I don't even remember going by the school as one of my errands."

"Tell you what. For the next hour while I give you the grand tour, let's not talk about what happened to you. Sometimes when you try too hard, your mind shuts down. No pressure here. It'll come to you when you're ready."

"That's just it. I am ready. I want this behind me. I want my normal, rather dull life back."

A few feet from the entrance into the stable, Luke stopped. "It's good to know you don't normally live all the time on the edge with men wanting to kill you." He swept his arm across his body. "After you, Meg—what name should I call you, so people don't suspect?"

"Kate. Kathleen is my middle name, but few people know that."

"Okay. Kate it is then."

Liliana led a beautiful, large dark brown Thoroughbred from a stall.

Megan came to a halt a few steps inside the stable. "That's Lightning Bolt! I saw him win the Triple Crown three lengths ahead of the second-place horse."

He leaned close to her. "Don't tell anyone, but I forgot to breathe when he ran that home stretch."

His nearness sent Megan's heartbeat racing. She was glad Luke was on her side. He gave her a sense of security, and he certainly wasn't bad looking. He carried himself with confidence, but there was no arrogance in his bearing.

Liliana walked the champion horse in their direction. She paused near Megan, a twinkle dancing in her eyes. "You look better in that wig than I ever did. I bought it when I thought I wanted my hair to be auburn, leaning more toward the redhead side. After wearing it for a few weeks, I decided I liked how I am."

Luke's sister had the same dark brown, almost black, hair he did. In fact, the two looked a lot alike, especially in the gray color of their eyes and dark, long eyelashes.

"It was a shock when I put it on, but it does change my appearance, so hopefully, no one recognizes me," Megan said.

"I heard you wanted to see Lightning Bolt. I was on my way to let him loose in his paddock." Liliana shifted her attention to Luke. "The farrier changed his shoes."

"That ought to keep him for a while." Luke took the reins from Liliana. "We'll take him to his pasture."

"Thanks. I don't want to be late for my date."

Luke raised his eyebrows. "Date? This is the first I've heard about you dating anyone."

Liliana settled her fists on her waist.

"You may be my big brother, but you are not my keeper."

He laughed. "I know how to rile you. You're a grown woman and can certainly choose your own date, but I can still check out the guy when he comes to pick you up. We're a small family."

"Not this time. I'm meeting him in Lexington at the horse sale at Keeneland."

"Who is he?"

"Our vet, and it really isn't an official date. I just wanted to see your reaction."

Megan enjoyed the teasing exchange between Luke and his sister. She'd lost her sister so long ago, she'd forgotten what it was like.

"Bye, y'all." Liliana headed for the exit, stopped, and twisted around. "When I was putting the load of wash in earlier, I found a ring with two keys on it. They were in your jeans' pocket. I left it on the table in the laundry room."

Keys? To what? The school and her classroom? When she saw them, she should know—she hoped. "Thanks. I'll get them later."

Megan slowly placed her hand on Lightning Bolt's neck and stroked the big, dark brown stud. When she stopped patting the stallion, he looked back at her and nudged her arm.

"He likes you. You found the special spot he enjoys being rubbed."

"He's a beauty."

"Shh." Luke grinned and winked. "Don't let him hear you. He's all male. I don't want him thinking otherwise."

"Then he's handsome. Is that better?"

"Much better." Chuckling, Luke walked toward the rear exit, passing and nodding to an employee in a stall.

"Who's he?" Megan asked when they stepped outside.

"My foreman, Malcom Wright. He worked for my dad, and I was thrilled when he said he would stay on when my parents turned over the farm to Liliana and me. His presence allows me to leave when Shep and I are needed for a search and rescue." Not far from the stable, Luke opened a gate to a field and released Lightning Bolt.

As the stallion trotted off, Megan

scanned the other paddocks. "Are all of these for stallions?"

"Yes. Most of these horses are part of my stable, but there are a few that are boarded here. I have another barn where I keep my horses that are still racing. Slowly I'm changing over totally to a stud farm."

Megan gestured toward a big red stallion in the field next to Lightning Bolt. "Who's that?"

"Red Clover. He's been retired for years and his lineage has proven to be excellent. His son won the Kentucky Derby this year."

Megan covered the distance to another paddock where a white horse loped along the perimeter. "He's—handsome. What's his name?" She leaned against the wooden slats, painted black as all the fences were at Riverdale Farm.

"Snow Storm." The stallion stopped, looked at them, then turned in their direction and charged forward. Luke clasped her shoulder and pulled her back. "He's temperamental and a loner."

Snow Storm veered off to the right. Megan watched him, her heart thumping against her ribcage. When she turned toward Luke, she caught sight of a vehicle coming toward the stable—a sheriff's car. Her pulse raced, and sweat beaded her forehead.

FIVE

Why was Sheriff Clinton coming to Riverdale?

Luke strode toward the front entrance into the stable. He hated leaving Megan alone outside the back door, but he didn't want to test her disguise. Right before he'd left her, she gripped his arm and told him in her dream that the man leaving the women's restroom at school had been dressed in navy blue slacks and a short sleeve shirt like a Sweetwater City police officer. She couldn't remember if he wore a gun belt or not. But Luke didn't want to take any chances until he knew more of what was going on.

He put on a neutral expression and shook hands with the sheriff. "What's brought you to Riverdale?"

"I got a call from the police chief in Sweetwater City. A neighbor said you came by Megan Witherspoon's house and ended up taking her dog that you found out back."

"Yes. Louise told me about the fire, that a body, tentatively identified as Megan, was found inside, and that Lady was missing. I searched for the poodle and found her cowering under a group of bushes. I didn't want to leave a dog homeless. Why in the world would the police chief send you out here for Lady?" Especially since Chief Franklin knew Luke's phone number and could have called himself. "Megan was a friend, and I was stunned to hear about her house burning down."

"How did you know Megan?"

"We met on a rescue. She loves dogs like I do, and we hit it off. I dropped by to see how things were going." Luke met the sheriff's gaze to gauge any reaction to his next question. "Have the police learned anything new about the fire, the body found?"

"The body in Megan Witherspoon's house fits her height and other indicators like a ring she was wearing. Her car was in the garage, but there's another missing woman in Sweetwater City. She's of similar height to Megan. The police are trying to ID the body to make sure it's Megan, so they're chasing down any leads."

Luke's gut tightened. "Who's the other missing woman?"

"The school nurse, Shelly Baird. Her husband reported her missing early this morning. The last place she'd been seen yesterday was in her office at the school. Her car hasn't been found, and no one in town has seen her in the past twenty-four hours."

So probably the woman in Megan's house was the school nurse. Megan should be safe as long as the would-be killers thought she was at the bottom of the Kentucky River. "Shep is a good tracker. I'll call Chief Franklin and offer my services if he needs Shep's expertise."

"Thanks. I'm sure he'll appreciate it if there's a need. The police are looking for Shelly Baird's car. When they find it, maybe he'll need your dog. I was near here when I got his call, so I told him I'd swing by and see about Lady."

"I'll get in touch with him. I don't mind keeping her for the time being. My sister's already fallen in love with her."

Sheriff Clinton nodded. "Good day."

Luke stayed in the entrance until the sheriff's car disappeared. Then he swung around and started for the rear door but collided with Megan who had come up behind him. He quickly grasped her upper arms and steadied her. "I didn't hear you."

"Sorry. I saw the sheriff drive away. What did he want?"

For a few seconds, he wanted to pull her against him and wrap her in his embrace. To make sure no one harmed her. Instead, he released his hold on her and stepped back. "He thought I knew where you might be because I have Lady. Louise told the police about me finding and taking Lady, but I didn't tell her my last name."

"Louise is known for keeping an eye on the street, especially during the day when most of the people are at work. She might have jotted down your license plate number when you drove away."

"I wish she'd been that vigilant last night."

"So do I. I grew up in that home."

Her expression made Luke wish he didn't have to tell her what else the sheriff had said, but she needed to know. It might help her figure out what happened. "Your car was in your garage, and there's another missing woman—Shelly Baird."

Megan sucked in a deep breath, her color flushed from her face.

"Do you remember seeing her at school yesterday?"

She closed her eyes and dropped her chin. When she raised her head, she shook it. "The only memory is what I told you about my dream. I don't even know if that's right." She scrubbed her hand across her forehead. "Shelly is one of our school nurses. She's one of three for the main campus. I've seen her a couple of times this summer. While summer school was going on, she was usually on duty." As Megan stared over Luke's shoulder, she chewed on her lower lip. "Her office is in the administration building next to the elementary school. I don't know why she would be in the bathroom near my room yesterday. In fact, I thought I was the only teacher in my area. The halls were dark and deserted."

Luke came to Megan's side and slung his arm over her shoulder. "C'mon. Let's go back to the house. The news should be on soon. We'll see what, if anything, is said on the local station."

As they emerged from the stable, Luke made a slow sweep of the landscape. Everything seemed all right, but if the police knew he'd picked up Lady, that could mean Megan shouldn't stay here. What if an officer with SCPD heard about her dog coming with him? Who else could Louise have told besides Chief Franklin?

* * *

Megan sat next to Luke on the couch in the den as the local news came on the large flat-screen on the wall. When the newscaster began a story in Sweetwater City, Luke covered her hand with his. On the TV screen, Megan and another woman's photo was displayed.

"The Sweetwater City Police Department are looking for two missing women: Megan Witherspoon and Shelly Baird, both employees of the school system in their town. If anyone knows the whereabouts of these two women, please notify the police at the number on the screen. If anyone has seen a white 2016 Saturn S-Series with the license plate number on the screen, please contact the police. They think foul play is involved in their disappearances. Megan Witherspoon's house burned down last night shortly after nine o'clock. An unidentified woman's body was found among the rubble. Please come forward if you have any information about the fire."

As the newscaster moved onto the next topic, Luke clicked off the TV. "After the visit by the sheriff today, my connection to you has been revealed. Granted the thugs who tossed you off the bridge think you're dead. But we may still have visitors come to check out the farm. I think it's time for you to move to another place. I know of a cabin, not too far from where we were that I can use. I also think we should contact Chief Franklin and meet with him away from the police station."

"No! What about my dream?" She tried to picture the man walking away from the women's restroom. Too vague to know if he was a police officer with the SCPD. "I don't know for sure, but every time I think of talking to the police, my stomach clenches and my heart races. I don't know why, but…" Her throat closed around the rest of the words she wanted to say. Just thinking about the dream left her shaking. She hugged her arms against her chest.

Luke touched her chin and drew her head around. Their gazes embraced, such a tender expression in his eyes that she felt a wave of calmness ripple through her. "I won't do it if you don't want me to," he said in a soft voice. "We can revisit it later. Because of the rough terrain, we should leave right before dawn tomorrow. By the time we get there, it'll be light enough to hike to the cabin. We'll use Liliana's truck in case someone's on the lookout for my SUV. Lady should stay here with Liliana, but I'm taking Shep."

"I agree. She isn't trained like him."

"If nothing else, he'll alert us if someone comes near the cabin."

"Whereas Lady would alert everyone within a mile's radius of the place." She attempted a smile that failed.

"I wish we could get into your school building and check the restroom near your room. It could help you remember if anything happened in there."

She stiffened at the thought of going inside the bathroom. "What if my dream isn't real?"

"Then we can rule it out. Our minds can play tricks on us. But that would mean letting Chief Franklin in on what occurred unless you have a key to the building."

She usually put her two keys—one to

the entrance and the other to her classroom—into her pocket. That had to be what Liliana was referring to earlier. Megan surged to her feet. "Where's the laundry room? I think the keys are in there on a table."

Luke rose. "Let's go see. Nadine should have dinner ready before she leaves for the guesthouse on the farm."

Earlier in the day, Megan had met Nadine, an older woman who had worked for the Michaels' family for twenty years. She ran the house and supervised two maids who came in twice a week to clean. According to both Luke and Liliana, Nadine was a great cook, and if that was all she did, they would still keep her as an employee. But she did much more than that—like a family member.

In the kitchen, the short, petite woman in her late forties turned from stirring something in a big pot—it smelled like beef–to face them. "I can tell something's wrong. Was it the visit by the sheriff?"

"Yes. He's looking for Megan," Luke said as he moved further into the room. "I didn't want to put you in the middle of this, but the police in Sweetwater City are looking for her."

Nadine's eyes grew round. "Oh, my. What's going on?"

Luke gestured to the table. "Sit down. I'll explain while Megan goes to the laundry room for her jeans and shirt. Have they been cleaned?"

"Yes, and ready to go upstairs."

"Megan can take care of them while we talk." Luke glanced back at her, silently conveying he wanted to tell Nadine the news.

Megan trusted his judgment and nodded. She left to pick up her clothes and take them to her bedroom. The past thirty-four hours had bled away her energy. She wished she'd slept longer. Would she even be able to tonight?

After Lady greeted her with licks, she scooped her dog into her arms and sat on the bed, needing some quiet time to think. She closed her eyes and lay back on the coverlet with her poodle snuggling against her.

If only she could remember the face of the man she thought she'd seen leaving the women's restroom in the dark hallway. She couldn't shake the feeling that he was a police officer and that was the only reason she didn't want to talk to Chief Franklin. Everything in her life was clear except the past thirty-four hours. She even remembered she had an apple with peanut butter for breakfast before she left the house on Thursday. Her eyelids slid closed while she delved deep into her memories. What did she do after that? Her mind went blank.

Frustrated, she opened her eyes and held Lady above her. The sight of the red of her dog's collar grabbed her attention. An image materialized in her thoughts—her hand flat against a door as she slowly pushed it into the restroom and automatically flipped the light on. A few feet inside, she froze, her gaze seized by the pool of blood in front of her.

SIX

After dinner with Megan and Liliana, Luke excused himself and went to his home office. He needed to make a few calls since he and Megan would be leaving for the cabin early tomorrow morning. His sister and foreman would take care of the farm and any business that came up. It wouldn't seem odd to anyone that he would be gone because he often left for days or weeks at a time. He'd wished Megan could stay at the farm until the case was solved, but the visit by the sheriff earlier still bothered him.

First, he called Lieutenant Clay Moore of the Kentucky State Police. They had grown up together and had been friends for most of their lives. If he could trust anyone, it was Clay, and Luke needed help. It wasn't about his safety but Megan's.

"What do I owe this call to?" Clay asked with a chuckle. "Boredom?"

Luke smiled. "Definitely not that. Remind me never to confide in you again."

"You're the one that decided to retire at the old age of thirty-three."

"Just from my first job. Did you ever imagine me working on Wall Street for a long time?"

"No. So what's up?"

"I need your help. Can you come over tonight? I have someone I want you to meet."

"A woman?" Clay asked with a laugh.

"Yes."

"You're kidding! You're dating again? I thought I would never hear you say that. Who is it?"

Good thing Clay didn't see Luke roll his eyes. "Just come over, and you'll find out who. It has to do with what's happening in Sweetwater City the past couple of days."

"I'll be there in half an hour."

After disconnecting with Clay, Luke punched in Chief Franklin's cell phone number.

"You never told me you knew Megan Witherspoon," was the first thing out of Joe's mouth when he answered the call.

"Only casually."

"You came by and took her dog. That doesn't sound casual to me."

"You know how I feel about dogs. Someone needed to take Lady, especially if Megan's dead. That's what you believe, isn't it?"

"Maybe. But nothing official yet."

"What in the world is going on? Sheriff Clinton didn't tell me much when he came by the farm earlier. Do you need Shep and me to help with a search?"

"If we find Shelly Baird's car, yes. Right now, we don't know her last whereabouts. She was supposed to go to Lexington, or at least that's what her husband said. I'll keep you and Shep in mind if we need a search dog."

Something didn't feel right. Joe's voice

sounded strained. But the police chief wasn't used to having one dead body in a burnt house and another woman missing. "How about for Megan?"

"Everything points to the body in her house being her."

"What was the cause of the fire? The news report didn't say anything about that."

A long silence greeted Luke.

"Joe?"

"It's because the fire chief suspects arson. He's not sure, so I didn't want that reported until he comes to a final conclusion. I expect you to keep that to yourself."

"Of course. You have one woman possibly murdered and another missing. For Sweetwater City that's a big deal."

"Yeah. The last murder here was over a year and a half ago."

"If you need us, call. I'd like to help, especially since I was acquainted with Megan."

Luke ended the call with Chief Franklin, not sure if he could trust the man or not. At this point, he couldn't take a chance. At least he hoped Clay could help Megan.

A light rap on his office door drew his attention. "Yes?"

Megan entered the room with his dog at her side and closed the door behind her. All color drained from her face, she made her way to the chair in front of his desk. "I think I saw Shelly's dead body on the school restroom floor on Thursday."

"Think?" Luke skirted his desk and took the chair next to Megan.

She nodded. "I was trying to remember something to help me figure out what happened during that twenty-two hours when I lost my memory. A vision popped into my mind. I pushed the door open to the restroom and turned on the lights. That's when I saw her on the floor, her throat slit, blood pooling on the tiles. I turned to get help…" Her voice trailed off.

He clasped her hand to get her attention. "And? What happened?"

"I don't remember. I think I was knocked out." She touched the left side of her head. "It's sore and tender to the touch. I thought it was because of being tossed off the bridge, but I don't think that's it." She lifted her thick, heavy hair to show him the wound.

He frowned. "That could have been made by a butt of a handgun."

"My body hurt all over, so I didn't think too much about it until I took off the wig and looked in the mirror a while ago."

"If Shelly was killed in the bathroom, as you think, then there should be forensic evidence to that fact. I have a good friend, a lieutenant with the state police. He's on his way here. I've known him all my life, and I trust him. Maybe he can go to the school and check the restroom for any evidence."

"He knows I'm here?"

"Not yet. We need help figuring this out, especially if we aren't going to see Joe Franklin."

She shuddered when he said the police chief's name.

He clasped her hand between his. "I'll keep you safe. Clay can investigate for us and help us figure out what's going on. It won't be long before Chief Franklin figures out the dead body in your house isn't you."

"It could be Shelly. We're about the same build with blonde hair. If they put her in my burning house, it's because they wanted the police to think I murdered her and disappeared. Case solved."

"That's what I think, too."

The doorbell chimes resonated through the house.

He stood. "That's probably Clay. Stay here. I'll bring him back here. If it isn't Clay, I'll get rid of whoever it is." He paused at the entrance to the room. "Shep, guard." He hurried down the hallway and into the foyer. After he checked to see who it was, he quickly opened the front door. "Thanks for coming, Clay."

His friend stepped into the house. "So, what's going on?"

Luke remained in the foyer. "I saved Megan Witherspoon's life this morning. Two men threw her off a bridge with her body weighted down with chains."

Clay rubbed the back of his neck with his hand. "No wonder you were eager to see me. Does she know who tried to murder her?"

"No. We've been talking in my office though. She's been recalling some images of what she thinks happened yesterday."

"Good. I've heard Chief Franklin asked for dental records to verify that the body found in Megan's home is hers. The arson expert just moments ago ruled the fire was deliberately set using gasoline, mainly in the area where the body was found. That's why dental records are about all they can use to make an identification. Neither woman ever had any broken bones. Nor did the burned victim, so that rules out that method."

Luke slowed his steps down the hallway to his office. "Who's feeding you this information?"

"Lieutenant Will Samson. Will's an excellent cop. I've worked with him on some task forces, and whenever I need information about Sweetwater City, he's the one I call. Don't worry, though. I won't tell him about Megan."

"Why did he give you information on

the case?"

"He was tasked with briefing me on the statewide search for the two women. I did offer to help if they needed me. What's got you worried?"

"When I spoke to the chief, I got a funny vibe from him. Usually he jumps at the chance to have Shep and me help him track a scent. Over the past couple of years, we've helped him in a number of situations, and we've been successful, but he seemed hesitant with this case."

"You've got an exceptional dog. By the way, where is he?"

"Shep's been staying with Megan, especially since the sheriff paid us a visit earlier. If there's any trouble, Shep will let us know." Luke led the way to this office.

Shep had his head in Megan's lap while she petted him.

She glanced over her shoulder at them, her gaze lingering on Clay. "Thank you for helping me."

"It's a pleasure to meet you and to help." His friend shook Megan's hand and sat in the chair where Luke had been earlier while he half leaned, half sat against the desk.

Luke filled Megan in on the progress in the case.

"The body in my house has to be Shelly." Megan continued stroking Shep. "I think she was killed in a restroom near my school room." She recounted part of what she'd told Luke earlier. "It's only a matter of time before the police figure it out. I'll be the prime suspect."

Luke gripped the edge of his desk, hating to hear the panic in her voice. "No, you won't. I saved you from drowning. I'm your alibi."

"Not for Thursday when my house was burned down. We didn't meet until this morning."

"Someone threw you off a bridge into the Kentucky River. You're a victim like Shelly." Luke looked from Megan to Clay. "Right?"

"Technically you can only speak about the time she spent with you today. Megan's right. She's a person of interest. She's in the middle of what's going on."

"Someone tried to murder her, and she thinks a police officer, or someone dressed as one, killed Shelly. Tell Clay what you remembered earlier."

Megan repeated what she'd told Luke about finding the dead body on the restroom floor. "It was Shelly. I never got a good look at the man who left the place. The only light in the hallway was at the end where there were windows by the door. All the classrooms were closed. Most of the fulltime staff take their vacation between summer school and the fall semester, so they were gone."

Frustration churned Luke's gut. "Clay, the restroom has to be checked. I know the body won't still be there, but there could be blood evidence."

"How are you going to explain that to the chief without telling him about Megan?"

"We aren't. Megan has a key to the building. We could go there early tomorrow morning while it's still dark. Then after that, Megan and I can leave for the cabin while you follow up on what we find."

"I don't want you two involved. Go to

the cabin, and I'll let you know if there's anything in the bathroom to support that Shelly was killed there."

Megan straightened in her chair and shook her head. "I have to see the place. I don't want to, but it might help me remember what happened to me. I need to remember."

Clay frowned. "You make a good point. Visiting the crime scene might jog your memory. In cases like this, I would go through the local police."

"We can't." Luke pushed off his desk and began pacing. "I don't like not telling Chief Franklin, but something doesn't feel right here."

"I agree. We'll bring him in when we know more." Clay stood. "Okay, Megan?"

She nodded and pushed to her feet. Shep did the same and came to her side. "We should meet at the elementary school on the main campus by five-thirty. What custodial staff there is in the summer will arrive by seven."

They walked toward the hallway.

"Is the cabin the one we used for

hunting?" Clay asked.

"Yes. I'm taking my sat phone so if you need to get hold of me, use that number. I'll text it to you. I'll be removing the battery unless I need to make a call. That way tracing us through it will be hard. Since I'll be turning it off, leave a message. I'll check it a couple of times a day."

"Let's hope you two won't be gone long." At the door, Clay shook Megan's hand again. "It was nice to meet you. If you remember anything about the vehicle those two men used to take you to the bridge or anything else pertaining to this case, let me know immediately. That includes you, too, Luke. If you remember the color, even that's a start."

Luke flashed back to the scene at the river as the men hoisted Megan over the side. "Black."

"And I know I was in a trunk, so it wasn't an SUV or a truck."

Clay grinned. "It's a start."

"I wish I had more. It's as vague as my description of the two men. I was too busy fighting to get away. I hope I can remember more, especially what they look like."

Luke held her hand. "You will in time. It hasn't even been a day since it happened."

When Clay left, Luke made sure the front door was bolted and then set the alarm. "I hope you don't mind if Shep stays with you and Lady in your room. You'll feel better, and so will I."

"As long as the two dogs don't take up the whole bed."

Luke laughed. "Shep can be a bed hog. C'mon. I'll walk you to your room and get Lady. I'll take both of them out." He bent down and rubbed his dog behind his ears.

When he reached the guest room, Megan picked up Lady and handed her to him. "Thanks for everything you've done for me. I still can't believe how much my life changed in less than two days. The police are looking for me. I never thought that would happen."

Cuddling Lady in his arms, he paused in the doorway. "Most people don't. Your life can change drastically in a split second."

"Scary. That makes me realize even

more how important it is to believe in the Lord. We aren't in control. He is, and for that, I'm thankful."

Luke refrained from replying. Instead he took both dogs downstairs and out into the backyard. He put Lady down, and she trotted off next to Shep. The light from the deck illuminated the area. Luke kept an eye on them.

What Megan had said about the Lord seeped into his mind, bringing back memories he'd tried to forget. Neither his money nor his prayers had been able to save Rochelle. He'd poured himself out, begging God to save her. But she died, leaving a void he didn't think he could ever fill again. He preferred to be in control.

Luke whistled for Shep. His dog loped toward him with Lady right behind him. At least during the past few years he'd been involved in search and rescue, the hole created by Rochelle's death was slowly filling. But he'd learned never to get that close to another woman again. Megan challenged that.

* * *

Stuck between Shep on one side of the bed and Lady on the other, Megan lay on her back, staring up at the canopy. She still wore her freshly washed shirt and jeans with the school keys in her pocket, too tired to get up and change into the pajamas Liliana had loaned her. A slither of brightness from the security lights outside taunted her to climb out of bed and close the drapery better, but the two dogs were finally settled, and she hated disturbing them. Instead, she carefully rolled to her side facing away from the window, leaving Shep stretched out along her back. Lady readjusted herself against her chest.

Exhaustion crept slowly through her, the adrenaline rush she'd been functioning on for most of the day subsiding finally. Sleep whisked her away...

A low rumble sounded in her ear. A wet tongue licked her cheek. She opened her eyes to find Shep hovering over her while Lady was in her face. The growl grew louder as the German shepherd nudged her with his nose then barked.

All remnants of sleep vanished, and Megan sat up. The sliver of light had changed—brighter.

Was it morning already? Then why didn't Luke wake her up?

She hopped out of bed and hurried to the window, shoving the draperies open. Below her, fire had eaten its way to the house and up the front.

SEVEN

Transfixed, Megan stared at the flames below, their yellow-orange color mesmerizing.

Shep barked repeatedly—the sound finally penetrating her daze.

Megan gasped and swung around. She grabbed Lady and raced into the hallway with Shep running ahead, yapping.

She stopped and looked up and down the corridor. Which room was Luke's?

The second she finished that thought, a door across from her flew open.

Hair tousled, Luke appeared dressed in his gym shorts and a T-shirt. "What's going on?"

Before Megan could say anything, the home's fire alarm screeched.

As she pointed back into her bedroom, Liliana rushed out into the hallway from the room next to Megan's, yelling, "Fire out front. I've called 9-1-1 and Malcolm. He'll rally whoever's at the farm to fight the fire."

"We've got to get out of here. Heel, Shep." Luke hurried toward the staircase.

Her heartbeat pounding, Megan clutched Lady against her chest and followed Luke with Liliana next to Megan. Was this blaze caused by the same person who burned her house? Probably. Which meant whoever was after her had found her.

At the top of the stairs, Luke stopped. "How bad is the fire outside?"

Thick smoke filled the downstairs foyer with tentacles snaking their way up to the second floor. Coughs racked Megan as she turned away from it.

"From what I could see it was set along the front of the house," Liliana said.

Luke pivoted and shoved open the door

to the bedroom nearest the stairs along the back of the house.

Megan glanced over her shoulder and gestured toward the first floor. "I see flames. The fire has reached the entry hall."

Luke reappeared in the corridor. "So far the back is fine. We can't go down the stairs. We'll have to escape out a window along the rear of the house. Now. It's spreading fast."

Each breath Megan took in was filled with more smoke than the one before. "Do you have any rope?"

"Yes. Let's go back to my room. It's with my camping equipment I keep there." Luke retraced his steps to his bedroom. "Liliana, close my door and cram clothes or something like that under it. I'll get the rope. Megan, open the window and make sure the fire hasn't reached that area." He headed into his walk-in closet.

Liliana stripped the top sheet off the mattress and shoved it under the door. "There. That should help."

After putting Lady in a nearby chair,

Megan unlocked the window, lifted it up, then clutched the sill and leaned out slightly to assess the back of the house. The drop was about fifteen feet down. Sweat popped out on her forehead, and her breathing raced. She quickly stood back, trying to convince herself that fifteen feet off the ground wasn't that high.

She didn't see any flames, but plumes of smoke from the sides of the house billowed and began to roil across the yard below. The sound of sirens vied with the crackling of the fire. "So far the back is still okay."

Luke joined her, having donned jeans and a T-shirt. "I've tied one end around a leg of the bed. It weighs about seven hundred pounds, so it should hold. "Liliana, you go down first then Megan. As soon as she's on the ground, Liliana get help. While she's doing that, Megan, I'll send Shep down. After you untie him, I'll climb down with Lady in a backpack."

Luke put on leather gloves and secured the rope around Liliana. Then after looping it around his waist and bracing himself, he slowly lowered her to the ground.

He glanced over his shoulder at Megan. "It's your turn."

"I guess this isn't the time to tell you I'm scared of heights."

He chuckled. "Right. Just hold onto the rope. I'll do all the work. You can close your eyes."

Megan scooped up Lady from the nearby chair and hugged her. "You do what Luke wants. I'll see you in a minute."

Luke took the poodle, put her in a backpack, then fashioned a harness around Megan. Like Liliana, she backed out of the window, her feet dangling while she clung to the windowsill with both her hands.

"You have to let go, Megan. I've got you. I won't drop you."

She wanted to release her grip, but she couldn't make herself do it.

He leaned down and whispered, "You're safe."

"The fire has reached the den. We don't have a lot of time," Liliana shouted.

God is with me.

A loud crash startled Megan. Her left

hand slipped from the ledge, her body swinging to the right. The rest of her fingers slid off the sill, and she stiffened, preparing herself for a sudden drop. But she didn't fall. Luke slowly lowered her to the ground.

Megan quickly untied the rope. "Send Shep down."

Her gaze darted to the den window nearby. The flames inside illuminated the smoked filled room on the backside of the house.

"I'm going around front and let the firefighters know we're all safe." Liliana hurried toward the side of the house.

Shep reached the ground as Liliana disappeared around the corner.

Megan untied him. "Hurry, Luke. The fire's spreading fast."

"I'm coming now."

As she watched Luke make his way to the ground, Megan's attention bounced between the den window and him. Out of the corner of her eye, she spied a large man, not dressed as a firefighter, hurrying toward them from the rear of the yard. She tensed, her heartbeat racing like a Thoroughbred competing in the Kentucky Derby. Luke hung a few feet above her head.

"We've got company. To the right." Megan coughed, the smoke thickening around her.

"Shep, guard Megan."

His dog moved closer to her.

Luke let go of the rope and dropped the last six feet to the ground. As he straightened, he turned toward the man still in the shadows and stepped in front of Megan. Tension pulsated off Luke.

Megan unzipped the backpack and removed Lady who shook. "You're okay now." At least she hoped that was true.

When the man neared, Luke sighed. "That's an employee, Bud Roberts. He must have still been at the broodmare barn." He met the man halfway.

Megan couldn't hear what the two said. She started for the pair when a group of firefighters came around the corner with Liliana. Megan froze. More sirens resonated through the air. It wouldn't be long until she would be discovered.

* * *

Luke took a look at the firefighters heading toward Megan. He needed to get her out of here. The manager of the broodmare barn was a long-time employee whom Luke trusted, and right now, he needed someone like that. "Bud, will you do me a favor?"

"Sure, boss."

"Can you take my guest to the office in the broodmare barn? She's been traumatized enough."

Bud smiled. "No problem. Then I'll come back and help."

"No. Stay with her and make sure there aren't any strangers hanging around the barn. I think this fire was set intentionally. I want her safe. Shep will go with her." Luke gestured to Megan to come to him. When she joined him, he introduced her to Bud as Kate. "Bud will go with you and Shep to the broodmare barn. I'll be there as soon as I can."

Megan turned and called back to Luke.

"I appreciate this. Thanks."

Luke waited until they disappeared from view before he headed in the direction of the firefighters and Liliana.

His sister hurried to him. "Where's Megan going?" she whispered.

"Bud's taking her to the broodmare barn. I need to get Megan out of here unseen. Can you handle the police and firefighters? I have some other camping equipment in my car. I'm taking your truck and leaving. I'll call you later to see about the fire. I have a feeling it was started on purpose. You need to go stay with Uncle Ben in Lexington." Their uncle was a retired Marine general who would know how to protect Liliana until Luke could figure out what was going on. Until then, he needed to get far away from his family and protect Megan.

"What's going on here?" Liliana asked.

"Good question. It's got to be something big. One person, maybe more, have been killed over whatever Megan stumbled across, and I don't want her added to that list. Hire guards to protect the farm, especially the barns."

"I will. I'm staying here with Nadine in the guesthouse. I saw her out front. I'm thankful it wasn't windy, and that the detached garage and other buildings on the farm, especially the ones around the house, are safe." Liliana pivoted toward the rear of their home.

Luke reached out and grasped his sister's hand. "Don't stay. Go to Uncle Ben."

Liliana lifted her chin. "I'll be fine. Remember I'm hiring guards for the farm. One of us has to be here."

"But..."

Liliana's narrowed eyes, daring him to disagree, underscored the fact she wouldn't do what he wanted.

He searched for another plea for her to leave. "The house can be rebuilt."

"But we grew up here. All the memories—" Liliana's words came to a choking halt.

"We'll be okay. We'll still have our memories," he tapped his temple, "in our thoughts." He released his hold on her. "I need to get out of here. I'll be in touch." He hugged her then headed toward his SUV.

His hasty plan to use his sister's truck wouldn't work because of the mass of people nearby and the fact her pickup was white. He needed to get away without anyone seeing him. Instead, he carried what he could out of the side entrance to the garage away from the house and people. He headed to the broodmare barn, put his gear down just inside, and then went back for the last part of his camping equipment. When he arrived for the second time, he found Bud and Megan in the office.

"Bud, I'd like to use your truck. I have the keys to Liliana's truck, and you can use that."

"Your sister's okay with the trade?"

"Yes. As you saw tonight, someone isn't happy with me. Kate and I need to get out of here unseen. Your truck is black. It'll work. If anything happens to it, I'll replace it with a brand new one."

"I think I got the better deal here. Sure. You can take mine."

"Thanks." Luke turned to Megan.

"Ready to leave?"

She nodded. "What do I do with Lady?"

"Bud, Liliana will be taking care of Lady. Shep is going with us. My sister will be staying with Nadine."

The broodmare manager stood. "I'll take good care of them and the horses."

"I'm hiring guards to protect the farm."

Megan hugged Lady then handed the poodle to Bud. "I wish I could say she was like Shep. She isn't. She has a mind of her own."

"I've dealt with head-strong animals." Bud gave Luke a set of keys.

He passed Bud the one to Liliana's truck then turned to Megan. "Let's go."

After he covered the taillights, he started for the cab. A sense of someone watching him shivered down his spine. Hand on the driver side's door, he surveyed the area around him. For a second, he thought he'd glimpsed someone ducking behind the side of the barn. He took a couple of steps in that direction, stopped and went back to the truck. His priority was to get Megan out of here.

Quickly, he settled behind the steering wheel and handed Megan a pair of night vision goggles. "Hold this for me until I need it."

"You aren't going to use the headlights?"

"There's no sense in calling attention to us as we leave." He started the engine and pulled away from the far side of the broodmare barn. "I'm using the back entrance. I hope no one's watching that route since it isn't used much."

"You can really see with these goggles?"

"It's a weird greenish landscape, but yes, it works."

"Why do you have night vision glasses?"

"It allows me to search for a person after dark. That's been the difference between life and death for a couple of the people I've found." Now that he was away from the lights and fire, he took the device and put it on. "It took some getting used to."

"Where will we end up?"

"On a gravel road that leads to a paved one. It's not utilized much."

"Are we going to the school then?"

"Yes, we'll be there well before Clay, but that way I can case out the area." He glanced toward Megan. "I'll let Clay know about the fire although he might have already been informed about it."

"I'm surprised he hasn't called you."

"I took the battery out of my phone. I don't want anyone to track us by it." He rounded a bend in the road.

A large horse stood in the path.

"Hang on." Luke slammed on the brake. The truck fishtailed and headed straight toward the animal.

* * *

Megan barely made out a black shadow moving across their path. A horse? As Luke swerved the truck, she closed her eyes and braced herself for impact.

The vehicle came to halt. One eyelid slowly lifted then the other. Darkness surrounded them. "What happened?"

"One of my horses got out of its paddock. Probably because of the fire."

Megan swung her gaze from the windshield to the window next to her. "Where did it go?" She fumbled for the handle.

"Don't open the door. The light will come on."

"Once I get my phone working," Luke twisted around and grabbed something from the floor behind Megan's seat, "I need to call Bud and let him know about the horse. There may be more running loose."

While Luke made his call, she relaxed and looked in the direction of the main house. In the distance, the fire glowed in the sky. She'd brought this to Luke and his farm, and she couldn't even remember why someone wanted her dead. Maybe she should turn herself into the police. Then at least Luke would be safe.

He ended his conversation with Bud. "Several horses aren't in their paddocks."

"I'm sorry. I didn't mean for anything like this to happen to you. Instead of going to the school, take me to the Sweetwater City Police Department."

Luke started the truck. "No! You can't.

Someone came to the farm and set the house on fire just like yours. Other than your neighbor and the police, no one else knew about a connection between you and me."

"That's why I need to distance myself from you. I don't want anything to happen to you or your family."

"I didn't save you, so someone can kill you later. We need to go to the school, check the restroom, then hide while we figure out what's going on." Luke came to a stop. "Do you think if you distance yourself from me that will end me being in danger? They have no idea what you've told me. They wouldn't take the chance. We're in this together now."

Together. Not alone. That was appealing to Megan, yet how could she forgive herself if something happened to him? "Your house is destroyed because of me." She couldn't shake that thought. "I've tried not to harm others, especially children. Instead I want to help them."

"You haven't harmed me." He reached over, took the gate opener clipped to the visor, and pressed its button.

In the dark, she could barely see the gate, let alone if it was opening. Like with the horse, she only spied a dark shadow moving in her line of vision.

He drove forward and turned onto the gravel road, stopping only long enough to make sure the gate closed behind them. "We have several hours before we're going to meet Clay. Do you know somewhere we could stay undetected near the school?"

"The park near the lake. It's five minutes from the main campus. But really, you can take me to see Chief Franklin. I don't want anything to happen—"

"There's nothing you can say that will stop me from trying to help you. I couldn't live with myself if something happened to you."

The finality in his voice robbed Megan of a reply. If someone needed assistance, she would do the same thing. It would be hard for her to walk away from a person in need.

"We have to figure out what's going on. Paying a visit to the crime scene might be a way to jog your memory."

"I hope so, too."

There was a part of her that wanted to go to the school and remember everything that happened, but there was a part that didn't. She was afraid of what she would recall. Could it be worse than seeing Shelly on the restroom floor dead? She'd known Shelly Baird as a nurse and member of the staff, but they weren't friends. Shelly had been a new employee of the district last year and someone she only saw in a professional capacity.

Once Luke arrived at the highway that led to her town, he stopped and got out of the truck. "Be right back."

Momentarily Megan thought about driving off and leaving him, but as though he'd considered that, he climbed into the cab less than a minute later.

He switched on the headlights and pulled out onto the highway. "I had tape over the taillights. I took it off."

The thought of Luke taking care of everything comforted Megan. But she kept her vigilance on the road for anyone that might be following them. Until they grew closer to Sweetwater City, their truck was the only vehicle. The closer they got to town, the more traffic appeared. Her tension increased.

Luke found a place in the park to wait for the time they were to meet Clay. From the street, the truck was hidden from view, and for the time being, she relaxed and leaned her head against her window.

"We have two hours. You should get some rest, Megan. Later, we'll need to hike up a mountain."

She scanned her surroundings. She couldn't see much but an occasional far-off light through the foliage. "I'll try. I'm exhausted but not sleepy."

"Come here." Luke drew her closer to him, his arm cradling her against him. "Since this old truck doesn't have bucket seats, stretch out as much as you can. Close your eyes and think of being in a bed in a safe place."

She chuckled. "That might test my imagination."

But his nearness lured her toward a sense of safety. The last thing she remembered was Shep moving around in the backseat. The thought of both of them guarding her whisked her into a deep sleep...

The sound of a bird tweeting floated to Megan and dragged her awake. For a few seconds, she couldn't remember where she was. Her cheek pressed against a leather seat. Her legs were curled up against her. Her surroundings finally registered as dim light filtered in around her. Bud's truck.

Suddenly she shot up and twisted around.

Where were Shep and Luke?

EIGHT

Luke looked through his binoculars in the predawn light at the back entrance into the elementary school. Everything appeared all right. But he couldn't shake the sensation he was being watched like at the barn. Although he left Shep guarding the truck outside, he needed to get back to it before Megan woke up. Clay should be here soon, and then they could get the visit to the possible crime scene over with. He'd feel better when they could disappear in the wilderness and hoped that Clay could figure out what was going on in Sweetwater City.

When he spied Clay's patrol car pulling

up to the rear of the school, Luke turned to go back to the truck. As he approached it, Megan thrust the door open and hopped down. Shep came up to her, wagging his tail. She bent over and hugged his dog. Luke moved toward her. She lifted her gaze to him, fear carved into her expression.

She shot up. "Where have you been? I thought something happened to you and Shep." Her loud voice rang through their hiding place.

He put his forefinger against his lips and quickly cut the distance between them. Leaning toward her, he whispered, "Sorry. I wanted to check out the school before we go there. I wasn't far away. You were safe with Shep."

"I thought he was with you." Her soft words still held the panic he'd seen in her eyes.

He certainly hadn't meant to scare her. He wrapped his arms around her and held her close. "I didn't want to wake you. You were sleeping so soundly." She felt good against him. They hadn't known each other more than twenty-four hours, yet she'd become important to him. "Clay's here. We need to go now. I'll feel better when we're out of Sweetwater City."

"Me, too." She pulled back and looked up at him.

He cupped her face. There was something about her that attracted him. "We'll get through this. You aren't alone. I have your back."

In the dim light from pre-dawn, Megan smiled.

It reached deep into his heart. His throat tightened. "Let's go." He looked down at Shep. "Stay. Guard." He opened the cab door for his dog to jump inside, cracked all the windows and then locked the truck. He didn't want anyone bothering the pickup while they were gone. Shep could appear ferocious when needed. "I don't want to keep Clay waiting." He took her hand.

At the street that separated the park and the main school campus, Luke panned the area around them, studying the shadows. Quiet reigned. He hurried with Megan across the road and into the rear parking lot by the gym. Clay exited his car and waited for them.

"You heard the news about Riverdale?" Luke asked as they headed toward the back entrance into the elementary school.

"You know I did. It's my job. Liliana's fine. Because it looks like arson, I called another state police officer in to deal with it. One of Zach's specialties is arson. I came here when Zach arrived at the farm. He's working with the fire department and the sheriff."

"Any questions about where I am?"

"Liliana told everyone that you're away. The sheriff asked where you were, but all she said was that you're on the road."

Megan dug into the pocket of her jeans, removed the key to the building, and inserted it into the lock. When she entered the school, she inputted the code on the security pad near the entrance. As they walked toward the restroom in question, Megan led the way. When she rounded a corner, the hallway before them was darker than the previous one. Luke glanced at Megan. Her mouth tightened. He wouldn't be surprised that memories must be assailing Megan concerning the last time she'd turned this corner.

"Now I understand why you didn't see the face of the suspect well." Luke walked beside her.

"My hall is the darkest one in the school." She came to a stop at a door with *women* written on it.

Clay moved to the door, pushed it open, and switched on the overhead light. "Let's see if we can find any blood residue on the floor."

Luke walked to the entrance while Clay sprayed Luminal on the floor.

Clay stood on the other side of the restroom. "Flip the light off."

Luke stared at a few places that glowed and glanced back at Megan. "Where was Shelly lying?"

"In front of the middle stall door."

"Take a look." Luke moved to the side to allow Megan to peer inside.

She remained where she stood several yards away from the restroom. "I can't!"

* * *

With her heartbeat thudding against her ribcage, Megan stared at Luke. She couldn't move forward. She wanted to, but her feet were rooted to the tiles as though blocks of cement were attached. Sweat coursed down her face and dropped to the floor. Tremors rippled through her.

Luke let the door shut, covered the distance between them, and took her hands. "Do you want to figure out what happened to you?"

She nodded, her chest rising and falling rapidly.

"Then we'll go together. I'm here for you. Clay is, too." Hands linked, he took a step backward.

But Megan didn't move. Her gaze zeroed in on the dark entrance. It taunted her. She squeezed her eyes closed, but in her mind, she still saw the black opening beckoning her. If she didn't deal with it, what happened would haunt her forever. She needed to find out the truth.

Megan looked at Luke and slid her left

foot toward him then her right one.

"You can do this."

Her steps leaden, she closed the space between her and the restroom. Luke pushed the door open and stood next to her as she peered inside. Her gaze riveted to the evidence of blood—Shelly's—on the tiles. "That's where Shelly was."

"Do you remember anything about Thursday morning?" Luke flipped on the light.

With words stuck in her throat, she shook her head. She'd never seen someone die like Shelly had, her blood pooling on the restroom floor.

"We need to leave before it gets too late." Slightly behind her, Luke laid a hand on her shoulder.

"I agree. I'll go see Chief Franklin about the crime scene." Clay made his way toward them, circling around where the blood evidence was.

Megan swallowed several times. "What are you going to tell the police chief?"

"I received a tip that Shelly was killed in the restroom. This scene needs to be processed. There may be other pieces of evidence."

"Good. While you do that, we're going to disappear. I'll call later to see what Chief Franklin said. Remember my cell phone will be disconnected."

They exited the school.

"Keep in touch at least once a day," Clay said.

"Will you check in on Liliana for me? I don't want to drag her in any more than she already is."

Clay nodded and opened his driver side door. "Hop in. I'll drive you to your truck. The longer you two are on the street, the better chance you'll be recognized. Whoever's behind this is willing to kill to stop you."

"When you go to see Chief Franklin, that could include you, too." Luke waited until Megan slid into the backseat before he sat in the front passenger seat.

"I know. That's why I brought in another state police officer."

Would that be enough? She didn't even know why someone would murder Shelly.

This kind of crime spree didn't happen in Sweetwater City. She closed her eyes and rubbed her fingertips against her temples. She'd hoped returning to the restroom would give her a hint at the very least to what happened—like why someone would murder Shelly—but her mind remained locked as tight as the gold vault at Fort Knox. Maybe she was trying too hard. Getting away from the town and the threat hanging over her head might be what she needed to remember. She hoped so.

God, I need You. Please help me to recall what went on Thursday.

* * *

Luke parked Bud's truck in the grove he'd used before when coming to the cabin near the top of the small mountain. This was as far as he could drive and a good place to hide the pickup. He and Megan would have to hike the rest of the way.

"Will the truck be okay here?" Megan asked as she opened the front passenger door.

"I've camped here several times and haven't had a problem. This is off the beaten track. A friend of my cousin uses it a couple of times a year. The rest of the time he's let us stay there when we want to get away from civilization."

"Then it's perfect for us." She jumped down to the ground while Luke exited the other side.

He let Shep out of the backseat. "We have a lot to carry. I want to do it all in one trip."

Megan looked up the mountain. "How far?"

"Around twelve hundred feet up the back side."

"We have to go around then up?"

Luke nodded while he let the tailgate down and hopped up into the bed. "I'll pass you our equipment and food."

"You brought a tent. I thought we were staying in the cabin." She took the canvas bag from him.

"I like to be prepared in case we need another place to stay. It's a small one, though."

"Someone might find us here?"

Luke gave her a backpack. "Like I said, I want to be ready for any kind of situation that might develop. I learned that while involved in search and rescues."

"You know my idea of roughing it is a two-star hotel room. I've never gone camping overnight. I've hiked, but that's the extent of my abilities involving the outdoors. And the only reason I've done that is because hiking isn't that hard. It's just like walking down the street."

He laughed. "Not some of the places I've hiked."

After the equipment and supplies were on the ground, Luke vaulted over the side of the truck and landed a few feet from Megan.

"You've got energy after the night we've had?"

"I love the outdoors. It invigorates me. We'll take it slow and easy up the side of the hill."

"It's a mountain. It's over a thousand feet tall."

Luke handed her the lightest backpack,

which she put on. "It's a tiny mountain compared to some I've climbed."

Megan smiled, her blue eyes lighting up. "Thanks for taking my mind off what's going on for a moment." She reached for the nearest duffel bag.

"Here, you take this one. It's not as heavy."

"But you have two that you're going to carry. The least I can do is take the heavier one. I can pull my own weight."

"Okay. I've learned not to argue with you over the small stuff." He couldn't believe it had only been the day before that he'd met her. After the ordeal she'd gone through, she'd been intent on helping him as much as possible. A lot had happened since his first encounter with Megan.

"I call that progress."

Luke shut the tailgate and locked the truck then pointed to Megan. "Shep, guard. Keep up with me. If I go too fast, tell me. Let's go. First, we'll hike around part of the hill—I mean mountain—then up."

In spite of little sleep and a traumatic couple of days, Megan kept up with Luke's pace. He didn't go nearly as fast as he would if he was alone. Earlier at the school he'd hoped she would remember the man she'd seen leave the restroom. They were back to square one. When he arrived at the cabin, he would call Clay and see what happened when he went to see Chief Franklin. Maybe there was progress on the case, and they wouldn't have to stay long on the mountain. He'd also have to contact Liliana. He hated leaving her alone to deal with the aftermath of the fire.

But right now, Megan needed him more than anyone else. He glanced over his shoulder at her. She was focused on the rocky path upward. When she looked up at him, her cheeks flushed. A thin layer of perspiration dotted her face. He couldn't take his eyes off her. Her breathing came out labored, but she uttered not a word of complaint.

"Let's take a break."

She lifted her head to peer up the mountain. "How much further do we have to go?"

"Not too far. But I could use some rest."

Margaret Daley

She grinned. "You don't have to pretend this is hard for you. But you aren't going to hear me complain about stopping for a few minutes." She slung her backpack to the ground and dropped to a leveled patch of grass. Shep sat next to her, and she ran her fingers through his fur.

On her other side, Luke settled near Megan, seeing the exhaustion in her face. The emotional upheaval she'd gone through the past two days could break a lot of people, but without complaint she kept going. She reminded him of Rochelle—delicate on the outside and tough on the inside.

He couldn't change the past. He shook away the memories of his dead wife, needing to stay focused on protecting Megan. He looked at her reclining back with her eyes closed. "Megan," he said in a soft voice.

She didn't move. Her exhaustion had overcome her. He studied her beautiful face with a sprinkle of freckles across her nose and a rosy tint to her cheeks. For a long moment, he stared at her full lips and wondered how they would feel against his. A light breeze blew a strand of her blonde hair across her forehead and right eye. He gently brushed it away, drawn to her calm, peaceful look in sleep as if those two men hadn't tried to kill her. But they had, and he had no idea who they were.

He lay on the grass next to Megan while Shep stood guard. Relaxing, Luke closed his eyes. His last thought as sleep whisked him away was what would kissing Megan feel like.

* * *

Even though she shook from head to toe, Megan laid her palm against the restroom door and pushed it open. When she stepped inside, she turned on the overhead light, illuminating the horror on the white tiles. The school nurse lay face down, blood flowing from a slit on her neck. From the amount of blood on the floor, Shelly had to be dead.

A scream welled up from the depths of her soul. A man had just left. Megan slapped her hand across her mouth to keep the scream inside.

Megan fumbled with her purse and finally managed to retrieve her cell phone from its depths. As she punched nine, a slight sound behind her alerted her that she wasn't alone. Before she had a chance to turn to see who it was, something struck her head. As the room swirled around her, she shot a look over her shoulder at the face of the head of the campus police, the metallic scent of blood added to the spinning room, nauseating her.

That was the last thing she remembered as she sank to the floor.

The next thing she recalled was waking up in the trunk of a car as it went over a bump, bouncing her against something in a plastic bag. She tried to move her hands to explore what was beside her. They were handcuffed behind her back. As she struggled to free herself, the vehicle hit another rough patch of road and bounced her continually against the plastic bag. The last pothole slammed Megan into the side of what felt like a face.

Shelly!

Fear strangled the scream inside her...

Megan bolted upright, her eyes wide.

Where was she? She scrambled to her feet, blinking at the brightness of the sun. She looked down. Shep sat, watching her.

That's right. We're on the side of a mountain.

She scanned the area. Where was Luke?

He's left me!

After the dream she'd had, panic blanketed her in a cold chill in spite of the warmth of a summer day.

Then she spied Luke approaching. She sank to the ground.

He rushed to her. "Are you okay?"

She shook her head. "Where were you?"

"I had to take care of business. I was just around that boulder. I was only gone a couple of minutes."

She bent her head, kneading her fingertips into her forehead. "I had a dream about what happened in the restroom. I don't know if it's true or my imagination."

"Tell me about it." He sat next to her.

His nearness calmed her tattered nerves. Her life had been routine and quite frankly dull. She worked, saw friends, and dated occasionally. Everything changed on Thursday, and she had no idea what was going on—until now.

She told Luke about the dream before she forgot it. "Why in the world would Keith Drummond kill Shelly? He's been the head of the campus police for several years. Before that he was a deputy sheriff."

"Are you sure it was him?"

"He was the one I saw in my dream, but I can't verify its validity. It's a dream, but the campus police uniforms are similar to the Sweetwater City police ones."

"When I call Clay, I'll have him look into Drummond. Did you ever see Shelly and him together?"

"Maybe a few times during the school year but nothing unusual." She paused, tilting her head in thought. "I also remember when I was in the trunk of the car right before I was tossed off the bridge, there were bundles of drugs in there with me. Lots of them."

"With Shelly's dead body?"

"No, a different time. When he stopped and opened the trunk, he gave me a shot, and I lost consciousness again. But at that time the trunk was only filled with me and Shelly."

"Did you see where he stopped?"

"There were lots of trees around, but I couldn't tell much more than that."

"Let's go." Luke rose and held his hand out to Megan.

She took it and stood. "How long did I sleep?"

"Over an hour but I have to confess I took a short nap, too. We're close to the cabin."

"Good because I'm starving. I've worked up an appetite."

He chuckled.

He started to turn around, but Megan reached out and stopped him. "Thanks."

He glanced back.

For a long moment, their gazes embraced across the small expanse that separated them. He moved closer and dipped his head toward hers. His mouth hovered above hers. Their breaths tangled. She wanted him to kiss her. Her lips tingled in anticipation.

Then he closed the space between them. The kiss, gentle at first, quickly evolved into much more. When he wrapped his arms around her and drew her to him, the shelter of his embrace wiped the remnants of her fear away. He'd lost so much trying to protect her. She didn't know how she could ever repay him.

NINE

Luke sat on a stone overlooking the valley below him while he placed a call to Clay. "We arrived at the cabin an hour ago. How's Liliana?" His sister was a strong, determined woman. He knew if anyone could take care of the mess created by the fire it was her.

"She hasn't stopped. It's official the fire was started intentionally. The sheriff is running point on the investigation, but I'm also looking into it with Zach Blackstock, the state police officer I brought in."

"Was the fire confined to the house?"

"Yes. It helped that it was calm last night. If a wind had been blowing, that might not be true."

Closing his eyes for a few seconds, Luke sighed. "When we were leaving the farm, we encountered a spooked horse. Is everything all right with the other animals?"

"All accounted for and uninjured."

"Good. Besides letting you know we made it, Megan believes the man who abducted her was Keith Drummond, the head of the campus police." Luke explained to Clay how Megan came to that conclusion and the fact drugs had been in the trunk with her when the two assailants took her to the bridge.

"So, it wasn't a Sweetwater City police officer and drugs might be involved somehow? Then it might be possible to at least bring Chief Franklin in on what's going on."

"I don't know if we should. If it's a drug ring, we don't know how wide it's spread. We have no idea who the two men were who threw Megan off the bridge."

"Could one be Drummond?"

He thought about what Megan told him

yesterday morning when she talked about the guys who tried to kill her. "Maybe. She only remembered seeing one of the men. She described him as tall and husky like a bodybuilder. He had dark hair and eyes. She didn't see the other one—at least she hasn't recalled what he looks like."

"I'll dig into this and let you know what I find the next time you call me."

"Was the woman in Megan's house identified?"

Clay didn't speak for a very long moment. "Yes. As we suspected, it's Shelly. The search for Megan has intensified. There's talk that she killed the nurse or she's dead like Shelly."

"Thanks for your help. Please let Liliana know we're okay. I'll call her and you tomorrow." As soon as Luke disconnected, he disabled the satellite phone, so no one could track their location.

With all that had happened to Megan over the past two days, she needed the rest. He'd encouraged her to take another nap with Shep by her side while Luke looked around and called Clay. But a rustling sound behind him sent him twisting around as he leaped off the small boulder, clutching his rifle.

Megan gasped, throwing up her hands. "I surrender."

"You're supposed to be sleeping."

She approached him with Shep by her side. "After counting a thousand sheep, I gave up. I'm still trying to process the fact Keith Drummond might have killed Shelly. I can't figure out why. Could he be connected to a drug ring?"

"Anything is possible. If we knew the answer, we'd know what's going on. Could Shelly have been involved with drugs? As a nurse, she would deal with them."

"I wish I could say. I didn't know her that well."

"At least Clay and his friend are working on it."

Sighing, Megan stared at the sea of green stretching out before them. "It's beautiful up here."

"Yeah. I enjoy coming up here when I can get away."

"Do you do it much?"

"No."

"I thought you were retired."

"Nope. I'll never retire."

One of her eyebrows lifted. "A workaholic?"

"Not like I was before. I was a driven man. Not anymore."

Megan took a seat on the boulder. "What made you retire from Wall Street?"

"My wife died. She loved New York City with all the hustle and bustle. I didn't. When she was gone, I had no reason to stay even if I had wanted to continue in finance."

"But you didn't continue?"

"For twelve years that was my life. It consumed me. After I buried Rochelle, I took a hard look at my life. When I started in financial planning, I loved my job. It was a challenge and exciting, but I also realized my wife and I rarely did anything as a couple. I loved her, and we'd grown apart. We were going in two different directions."

Megan brought her knees up against her chest and laid her head on them while clasping her legs. "How did she die?"

He stared at the bright blue sky, watching a hawk soar on an air current. He rarely talked about her death, but after what Megan and he had shared, it seemed natural to tell her. "One of the few vacations we went on was to a ski lodge in Vermont. Usually we went at least for one long weekend in the winter. Rochelle taught me to ski. She loved it. I tolerated it. The last time we went she was caught in a rare avalanche. I tried to save her. I..." Emotions crammed his throat. As memories inundated him, he dropped his head and swallowed several times. "I couldn't. I begged the Lord to save her, but He didn't."

"I had a younger sister who dove into a lake where she shouldn't have. She hit a large rock that was submerged and hidden from the shore. My dad and I went into the water to find her. The whole time I prayed to God to help me find Cara. I did, but she never woke up from a coma. She died after a few days. My parents divorced shortly after her death. It tore the family apart. I don't even know where my father is."

Luke took her hand. "I'm sorry. I know how hard it is to see that happen in front of you."

"I was angry at God for taking her and wouldn't come out of my room. My mom came to talk to me. I wouldn't listen at first. Then her words slowly seeped through my anger and grief. Not all of our prayers will be answered the way we want. God sees the bigger picture, and for a reason we might not understand, our wants weren't fulfilled. Things happen, and I might never know why. I learned I have to put my trust in the Lord. He knows best. The alternate is to be angry and bitter because I didn't get my way. We don't always."

Luke drew strength from Megan's words. *Has that been what I let happen to me?* He'd spent years blaming God. Rochelle's death was an accident. There was no blame, and even if there had been, what good was that for him? He was living in the past. Rochelle would never want that for him. "You've given me something to think about."

"I'm only passing along my mom's advice with a little of my own sprinkled in. I've been thinking about it a lot these past couple of days. I need to trust God even when things aren't going my way. Not always easy to do. When I was thrown from the bridge, that was all I could do—pray and trust." Their gazes connected. "And you showed up."

He smiled. "So, you think the Lord brought us together?"

"Yes."

He slipped his arm around her and slanted a look at her. "I think so, too."

He bent his head close to hers. His mouth hovered over her. The urge to kiss her swamped him. He leaned down and planted his lips on hers while drawing her against him. The feel of her in his embrace felt so right.

When he finally pulled back, he touched his forehead to hers. "I told Clay about Keith Drummond and the possible drug angle. He'll look into the man and let us know what he finds out. Hopefully we won't have to be here too long, but while we are,

I'm going to show you camping can be fun."

"That's okay. I'll take your word for it. Besides counting sheep and getting nowhere, I saw a big spider crawling across the ceiling in the cabin. Now I'm not scared of spiders like some people, but he was big." She raised her hands and spread them about a foot from each other. Clearly an over exaggeration.

"Oh, that's Fred. He was here last time I was. He's harmless."

"How do you know that?"

"Because nothing happened to me." He slid his arm along her shoulder, rose, and started toward the cabin.

"Are there any more critters that I should know about?"

"None that will hurt you. There's a small black bear that hangs around from time to time, but Shep will warn us. So long as we lock the door and keep our food and trash inside, he won't stay."

"A bear! How can you talk about him so casually?"

"I've been here a couple of times

before, and he hasn't threatened me. Besides, when I come up to the cabin, I always carry a gun." He brought the rifle up and slowly opened the door then panned the interior. "I think it's safe. Fred's gone, and I don't see any threats." He stepped aside and let her go inside.

"Ah, ha! There's a flaw in your reasoning. If it's safe, why do you carry a gun?"

"Because I always plan for the unexpected. It's best to be prepared rather than wish you had a weapon when something happens."

She held out her hand, palm upward. "Okay, then where's my gun?"

"Since the outdoors isn't your element, I figured you don't know how to use one."

"Gotcha!" She planted both fists on her waist. "My daddy taught me. He used to take me to the shooting range with him."

Luke moved closer. "I only have the one rifle, but I do have a revolver. I'll let you have it if you show me you can shoot."

"Which one?"

"That's up to you."

"Both. He showed me how to fire each kind."

Luke marched over to his belongings and picked up the revolver. "Let's go outside."

As he followed Megan, he was continually amazed by her. And after she shot each weapon a couple times, he was even more impressed. "But you don't like camping?"

She held the rifle, pointed downward. "They don't go together. Sleeping on the hard ground never appealed to me. When my dad wanted to rough it, he went with friends. My mom, my sister, and I always stayed home."

"Then I guess we aren't going to take turns sleeping on the cot in the cabin?"

"You're right." She grinned and winked at him. "While the cot isn't like my bed at home, it's much better than the wooden floor."

Among a cluster of trees near the cabin, a light wind cooled the hot air—slightly. "We have food, a roof over our heads, and one bed. Not too bad."

Megan leaned the rifle against the trunk and fluttered her hand in front of her face. "Too bad there isn't an air conditioner and for that matter, electricity."

"When the sun goes down, we'll use a couple of lanterns. We'll have light."

"Can we at least open the windows and get a cross breeze?"

"Yes. The first year I came in the summer, I asked my friend if I could install screens. Since then I've added a few other luxuries."

Megan's eyes grew round. "What? I didn't see any luxuries."

"The cot, cooking utensils, pans and dishes in the cabinet are mine. Also, the chairs and table. I didn't want to bring them up the mountain each time. Clay helped me that trip." He picked up the rifle then headed to the cabin and held the door for her to go inside. "I forgot the curtains over the three windows. That was Liliana's suggestion."

Megan chuckled. "Downright homey, but you aren't going to be able to convince me this is better than a hotel room."

"Wait 'til you see the sunset and sunrise from here and the joy of silence. But what I love the most is the sense of getting totally away from the rat race."

"I would like that from time to time." She sat in a chair, releasing a long breath. "I'm not ready to go back to work in a couple of weeks. All the things I saved to do in the summer and didn't get done, I..."

He took the seat catty-cornered from her. "What?"

"Everything I'd planned to do and clean out burned in the fire." Shaking her head, she clasped her hands on the table. "I haven't had time to process the loss." Her gaze fixed on him. "The same for you because of me. I've put you in the middle of what's happening to me. I appreciate what you've done for me more than any words can convey. But tomorrow we need to leave and return to Sweetwater City. Now that I remembered that the mystery man was the head of the campus police, I'm sure it'll be safe to talk to Chief Franklin."

He covered her hands with his. "No.

We'll wait until Clay has investigated Drummond, especially his connection to the drug angle. I didn't risk my life to save you, so I could leave you in danger and walk away."

"I hate people thinking I'm dead or a murderer."

He rose and drew her to her feet. "That's better than the alternative. I'm here to keep the dead part from occurring." He tugged her toward the door. "Let's go look at the sunset."

"Did you talk with Liliana?"

"No, but Clay said she's all right and no animals were hurt. The fire was contained to the main house."

"But all your possessions are gone."

Luke stepped outside and scanned the area. In the distance, the sun neared the hilltop to the west with bands of orange, yellow, and hot pink entwining in the blue sky among the clouds gathering. "I know, but they can be replaced. If something happened to you or someone else that would be completely different. When Rochelle died, I looked around our beautiful apartment that she had carefully and painstakingly created. She was very proud of our home. It meant nothing to me without her. In fact, I couldn't wait to sell it and live somewhere else. I was having a hard time moving on when I was constantly reminded of her."

"It was the house I grew up in. Lots of memories."

"Those are still in your mind, and you can rebuild in the same place." He swept his arm across his body. "What do you think?"

Making sure she didn't glance down into the valley, Megan finally looked toward the sunset and sucked in a deep breath. "Beautiful. I can see why you like to come up here."

Luke shifted his attention to Megan. "Yes, beautiful," he said, his gaze taking her in.

He tried to keep telling himself the only reason he didn't turn her over to Clay to keep her safe was because his curiosity had been aroused. But he felt responsible for her. For the first time since Rochelle's death, he couldn't stop thinking about a woman—Megan.

* * *

Megan snuggled under the light cover on the cot, the quarter moon the only light coming into the cabin through the window by the door. All the windows were raised and the curtains open to allow a cross breeze. Not far away, Luke lay in his sleeping bag while Shep was right next to her "bed."

Exhausted but wide awake, she curled on her side and stared into the dark at the hump on the floor where Luke was. The last man she'd dated seriously, a teacher at the high school, had broken her heart. They'd gone out for almost a year. He was supposed to pick her up for a date but didn't come to get her. An hour later, he called her and told her he wasn't interested in getting serious. He broke up over the phone. Later, she discovered he took another teacher with him to the high school football game that he and Megan were to attend. She heard through the grapevine he'd done the same thing to that teacher. She counted herself lucky now, but the rejection had hurt at the time.

Luke's kisses earlier made her think about Blake and the one thought that came to mind was she didn't want to be hurt like that again.

Shep jumped to his feet, barking. On the cot, Megan bolted up and looked around.

A scream came from deep inside her at the sight of a large shadow outside the window.

TEN

Megan's scream reverberated through the cabin, wrenching Luke from his sleep.

He shot to his feet, shedding his sleeping bag, and stooped to snatch his revolver from the floor near where he'd slept. "What's going on?" he asked over Shep's continual barking.

"Someone's at the window."

Luke whirled around and started forward. A large, shadowy figure rattled the screen as though determined to get inside. Shep darted past Luke and stood on his hind legs to get closer to the intruder.

A fierce roar rumbled through the flimsy

barrier between them and a big bear. In seconds the animal would have the screen dislodged, leaving a way into the cabin.

"Megan, turn on the lantern."

With his gun raised, he quickened his step and crossed to the animal. Light flooded the room, illuminating the dark brown eyes of the black bear as it swiped his paw across the screen, slashing it.

Before the animal climbed inside, Luke lunged forward and slammed closed the interior wooden shutters then dropped the board across them. He hastened to the other two windows and did the same while the frustrated bear protested.

"Can he get inside?" Megan asked as she hurried toward the rifle.

"Hopefully not. I think he's too big to fit, but I don't want to find out I'm wrong."

The bear rattled the shutters while Shep growled, his teeth bared.

Luke moved away from the windows and planted himself beside Megan. "Heel, Shep."

His dog gave one last snarl then came to Luke's side.

"I think I'd rather take my chances with Keith Drummond than our guest outside." Megan held the rifle as though she were ready to shoot if she had to.

"I don't think that's the same bear that usually comes around. He's a new one and seems bigger. I shouldn't have heated up the beef stew on the propane stove."

Their intruder pounded against the wooden barrier.

"I totally agree." Megan's grip on the gun tightened. "What if he doesn't leave?"

"He'll get bored and move on."

"What if he doesn't?"

He slanted a look at her. "We'll worry about that if it happens."

"How can you be so calm?"

"A lot of my search and rescues have been in the mountains and wilderness. I've learned to be prepared for all possibilities, respect the animals I encounter, and give them a wide space."

"How can you be prepared for all possibilities?"

"It's not easy, but I'm always learning new things."

Megan glanced at the window. "He's quiet. Do you think he's gone?"

"Maybe, but I'm leaving the shutters closed even if it gets stuffy in here."

She smiled. "You won't get an argument from me."

"Let's give it a while then try to get some sleep."

Megan eased down on the cot with the rifle on the bedding next to her. "Are we staying here tomorrow?"

"Where else can we go? We have people after us that burnt down your house and mine. The bear might be the lesser of two evils." As Luke finished speaking, a banging sound filled the cabin from the window near the front door.

Her eyes grew wide. "He's moved."

He sat beside her on the cot. "I shut the window on that one too, so it'll be hard to get in."

"If he's really determined, I think he could. He looked about six feet tall."

Luke wanted to take her mind off what was happening at the moment. He clasped her hand and scooted back to recline against the wall. "What do you enjoy about teaching?"

"I know what you're doing. I'm not going to forget the bear is there."

"Humor me. I really want to know."

"My favorite is the moment a student 'gets' something. Last year I had a little girl who had been struggling to read. Finally, things started to click, and by the end of the year she was reading nearly at her grade level. That was a highlight for her—and me."

"It sounds like your teaching is rewarding. That's the way I feel about helping people in search and rescues."

"When you give, it comes back tenfold." She twisted toward him, her blue eyes like two inviting pools on a hot day. "Honestly, without you helping me after you pulled me from the river, I don't think I'd be alive today."

"I'm just glad I was there to help you." For the past couple of minutes, it had been quiet outside the cabin. He hoped the bear was gone. He draped his arm over Megan's shoulders and tugged her gently against him. "Rest. I'll be right here, armed if circumstances change."

"What's the most memorable rescue you've been involved in?"

"The one early Friday morning."

She chuckled. "Besides that one, which I'm personally appreciative you were involved in."

As Luke told Megan about a couple of his search and rescues, her eyelids became heavier. Several times her eyes would pop open only to begin closing almost immediately. He schooled his voice to a monotone, hoping to lure her to sleep. He might not get any rest tonight, but he wanted her to.

The feel of her next to him, her head drooping against his chest while her arm rested across his stomach as she surrendered to sleep, produced an ache in his heart. He didn't want to care about her, but he did. The devastation after Rochelle's death had nearly destroyed him. He'd felt helpless and had turned away from God.

Lord, what are You trying to tell me?

* * *

Hours later when Megan opened her eyes, she stared into Shep's face, inches from hers. She laughed and ruffled the fur on his head. "Good boy." She pushed to a sitting position. The windows were wide open, and light flooded the cabin. "Where's Luke?" *Where's the bear?*

Shep barked when she said Luke.

Megan stood then finger-combed her hair as she crossed the room to the door and went outside. A cool morning breeze refreshed her. Stepping forward, she surveyed the area and found Luke on the rock where he'd been yesterday, talking on his satellite phone.

He glanced over his shoulder at her, said something to the person on the other end of the call, then disconnected it and took out his battery. As he stuffed the phone into his pocket, he hopped off the stone and faced her. His frown shouted that whatever he'd heard from the person on the other end wasn't good news.

She stopped in front of him. "What's

happened?"

"Keith Drummond was found dead early this morning in his car."

"How long had he been dead?"

"No more than an hour or two. There goes our one lead in the case."

"Did Clay tell anyone about Drummond?" Megan sank onto the rock, tired after being up for only minutes.

"No, but it's possible Clay alerted the wrong person to his interest in Drummond when he looked into the head of the campus police."

"Chief Franklin?"

"Maybe." Luke released a long breath, staring off into space. "We don't have any other leads right now. Clay's still going to dig into Drummond's life and a possible drug ring in the area, but he can't bring him in and interrogate him now."

"And if he has been murdered, then there are others involved who felt they had to silence him."

"I wish I could help Clay, but my one duty in this is to keep you alive. My concern now is how did Drummond's killer find out he was under scrutiny." Luke joined her on the stone.

"Maybe the killer murdered him for a different reason."

Luke kneaded his muscles along his nape. "Possibly. But I have to consider all angles. I've decided it might be better if we move to another place, especially with the bear paying us a visit last night. I saw his paw prints. He's big. Probably six hundred pounds."

"And he might return today or tonight?"

Luke nodded. "I looked at the damage he did to that one window. If he'd persisted, he might have found a way in, possibly by the door."

Megan shivered in spite of the warm temperature. "When do you want to leave? Where are we going?"

He touched the binoculars around his neck. "We can drive to another place then hike to a more remote location. I know of several further east of here. We should eat something then pack up and leave right away. I need to inspect the terrain below. There are several places where I have a good vantage point of the path up to this cabin and one area I have a partial view of the truck in the woods. Start packing our supplies while I look. Take Shep and close the shutters." After rising, he held a hand out to her, and she took it. He brought her up in front of him.

The memory of the kisses they'd shared sent goosebumps racing down her body. She couldn't remember anyone she'd dated who kissed as well as Luke. "I'll leave something out for us to eat. We're going to need the energy with all the walking we'll need to do."

"Agreed. It's easier going down the path than up. I'm glad you got some sleep last night."

"Did you get any?" she asked as she started toward the cabin.

"A few hours but I've gone without sleep during a few search and rescues."

As she paused in the doorway into the cabin, she looked over her shoulder at Luke. "Make sure wherever we go it's not bear country."

He chuckled. "Don't know if that's

possible." He started for a ledge obscured by heavy brush.

Inside, Megan quickly stuffed supplies into the duffel bags and backpacks. Most of their items were packed when she stopped to pull out energy bars and water for the hike down the mountain. Then she started looking at the food, trying to decide what they could eat quickly for breakfast.

Luke burst into the cabin. "We have to leave now! Three men are climbing up the mountain and one looks like your description of one of your assailants. Tall and husky with dark hair tied back. One was shorter, and the other I couldn't see well."

"If they're on the trail, how are we going to go down it without being seen?"

"We have to go down the other side. I can't say it's a trail like the one we used yesterday. It's steeper and part of it isn't really a path. We need to repack and leave what we can behind. We're only going to carry the weapons and the backpacks."

"How far away are the men?"

"Less than an hour. They haven't been

climbing long. We need to get to the bottom and to my truck—fast."

"What if someone's guarding the truck?"

Luke took out certain items in his backpack. "I'll deal with him. It's our only option. I'm calling Clay to let him know what's happening. It may take him a while to get here." He left the cabin to get a better signal.

As Megan reorganized her supplies, her pulse began to race. How was she going to get down a mountain without freaking out? On the trip up, she kept focused on the top. Now she would have to look at the bottom of the mountain, hundreds of feet below her.

* * *

Halfway down the mountain, the narrow ledge Megan clung to barely held her. If she put her heel down, it would hang off. The very thought of that kept her frozen in place on her tiptoes. The muscles in her calves protested. She should be reassured by the harness tied around her waist that connected her to Luke. But she wasn't. She stared at the stone facade inches from her face, not daring to look down at the ground below. Her heart felt like it was going to burst from her chest, its beating hammering so loudly in her head it took her a moment to realize Luke was saying something to her.

"We need to keep moving, Megan. Follow the path Shep and I took. It'll be easier when you reach the shelf. All you have to do is keep going."

Sweat ran in rivulets down her face, some stinging her eyes. "I wish I could traverse a mountain as well as Shep."

"He's used to doing it. You can do it. Move to the left for two yards. Then the area opens up wider."

Every second she hesitated narrowed the distance between them and the men who came to finish the job of killing her—and now Luke. She couldn't allow that to happen. Her fear of heights was all in her head.

She drew in a deep breath and slid her

right foot a few inches to the side, reluctantly prying her left-hand fingers loose from the rock jutting out. Quickly she clutched another stone hold while she drew her left leg closer to the other one. Now she had to repeat that motion—over and over.

The top half of the mountain hadn't been this steep and according to Luke the last third wasn't too bad. She kept that in her mind as she moved gradually lower. Scrapes and scratches covered her arms. At least her jeans protected her legs, but the heat from the sun drenched her from head to toe.

She paused a few seconds to remind herself to breathe deeper.

"You're almost here. Keep focused on where you're going, not below."

The temptation to see exactly where she was in reference to Luke taunted her just to take a quick peek.

No!

In this situation Luke knew what was best. When she made it out of this alive, she was determined to find a way to overcome her fear of heights.

"A couple of more feet."

The sound of his low, soft voice attested to his nearness. She chanced a glance to the side and saw the top of his head. The sight spurred her to move faster—which was a mistake. Her shoe slipped off, and she gripped the rocks tighter while she scrambled to right herself with Luke's help. He grasped her flailing leg and guided it back toward the ledge.

She kept going inch by inch until she neared the place where she could lower herself the few feet to the wide shelf Luke and Shep occupied. The second she did, Luke engulfed her into an embrace. She wanted to stay there, but her slow descent was eating up the time between her and the thugs coming after them. She had to remember that.

"You did it. The rest of the way is much easier. As we move down to the valley, walk behind me and keep your hand on my shoulder. Focus on me or your feet, not the terrain ahead of us. Okay?"

She pulled back and nodded. Her

parched mouth demanded water. She dug in her pack and withdrew a bottle of warm liquid. She didn't care. After drinking half of it, she passed it to Luke who finished off the bottle.

She placed the empty plastic bottle in her bag. "I'm ready."

Forty minutes later, Megan stood at the bottom and finally looked upward at how far she had come in an hour and a half. "I wish I had a camera. I'd take a photo of this. I'm here and I hardly believe I climbed down it."

"We'll come back one day and take a picture of it on the ledge in the middle to prove you did."

She chuckled. "That'll be the day."

"It's a goal to work toward."

The fact that Luke was talking about the future together revved her heartbeat as though she was still on the narrow shelf, grasping whatever she could to stay alive.

He signaled to Shep to follow near and slightly behind Megan. Sandwiched between her protectors, she walked in Luke's footsteps. Two days ago, she hadn't even known him and now her life depended on him.

Thank You, Lord, for sending him to me.

* * *

Luke left Shep guarding Megan in the thicket of underbrush in a ditch by the dirt road a couple of hundred yards back. He had to check to see if the people following them had found their truck and had posted one of the thugs to guard the vehicle. He crept toward the dark truck parked near the trail to the cabin but in an area hidden from sight off the dirt road they would have to take to the highway.

It had taken them longer to descend the eastern side of the mountain than he had hoped. They wouldn't have much time to get out of the area before the trio after them returned to their SUV. He'd disabled their car, so they couldn't follow them. And if he and Megan were lucky, the three guys would be here when Clay arrived.

As he neared the truck, Luke kept

panning the terrain around him. Through the green foliage he spied the black vehicle he and Megan had used. Aware of the gap closing on their head start, he moved quickly, his gun clutched in his hand.

A few yards away, he again paused to check for any signs of a guard. No one on this side. In case someone was on the other side, he hunkered down and ran toward it. As he stayed low and eased the driver's side door open, he looked from side to side. That was when he saw the two flat tires.

Luke circled the truck. All four tires were slashed. No way could they make a run for it driving it with only one spare.

He whirled around and ran back the way he came, branches slapping against his body. They had to find a good place to hide. It wouldn't be long before the men would return. When he emerged from the woods, he was only a hundred yards away from Megan. He focused on her, and the gap closed. He dashed across the dirt road, spying her not too far away.

A shot rang out.

ELEVEN

Abullet struck the dirt, mere inches from Luke's left foot. He dove for the undergrowth in the ditch on the side of the road where Megan hid. Another shot came from the direction of the mountain as he tucked and rolled. Megan returned fire with the rifle he'd left with her. He slammed into the hard ground, quickly unfolded his body, and withdrew his handgun.

He surveyed the trail up to the cabin. "Where are they?"

"Two are behind a boulder."

"Two?" he asked. "I saw three coming up the mountain."

"I've been following their progress, and

all I've seen is a large man and a smaller one."

"Did you recognize either of them?"

"It's hard to tell from this distance, but the large guy might be one of the kidnappers from the bridge."

Luke slanted a glance at Megan. "Where's the third thug."

"It's possible he's a little farther up the trail."

"Or below those two. There are parts of the path we can't see." Which worried him. His nape tingled as though someone watched him from behind. He peered over his shoulder and searched the terrain in the wide ditch and the ground above it on the other side. Nothing. When he switched his attention to Shep, nothing indicated his dog heard someone approaching from the rear.

"How did they know where we are?"

"I have no idea, but since they do, I'm calling Clay about what's going down. He needs to know the situation he's driving into." He dug into his pocket and withdrew the cell phone and its battery. He hurriedly inserted it and then turned his phone on.

When his friend answered, Luke asked, "Where are you?"

"About twenty minutes away with Zach and two state troopers."

"We're at the bottom of the mountain. The truck's been disabled, and we're pinned down by our visitors. How in the world did they find us?"

"Not sure. A good question to ask them when we apprehend them. Does Megan know any of them?"

After Luke told Clay about the large man, he disconnected the call. "He's close. We just have to wait. The mountain location has its good points and bad ones. I love the isolation, but that can be a problem, too."

Her gaze fixed on the vicinity of where the men were. "For the record, you have not convinced me going camping is something I would like."

He laughed, the sound strange coming from him in lieu of what they faced. But for a second, it relieved his tension. It quickly returned, though, knotting his muscles, especially along his shoulders. "You need to give me a second chance when we don't have people chasing after us and wanting us dead."

"Maybe. This experience may scar me for life."

"Give me a chance to persuade you."

"By the way, I owe Shep a steak dinner. His growl alerted me to get down, or I possibly would have been hit by the first shot."

Luke petted Shep sitting at attention between them. "Good boy. You're the best, and a steak dinner is definitely in order." When he returned his attention to Megan, he shook his head. "Why were you visible?"

"I didn't realize I was. I was trying to see more of the trail and must have popped up too far."

All he wanted to do was hug Megan and keep her safe. "We just have to wait for backup." He kept his attention on the mountain.

One of the men, thin and wiry, dashed from behind the boulder and lunged for the shelter of another stone on the other side of the path where the vegetation was denser—and possibly easier for him to move farther down the trail without Luke seeing him.

"Megan, you watch the guy behind the boulder. I'll try to keep track of the one on the other side."

"How much longer until Clay arrives?"

"Fifteen minutes. On the bright side, the thugs are trapped on the trail. I hope they give up when Clay comes."

"Lord, please protect us and end this today."

"Amen." Luke sighed. "I hope He's watching out for us."

"He is."

Megan's strong faith taunted him. He'd given up on God because he didn't get the answer he wanted. Life was full of trials and problems. They shaped people into the person they were. He remembered times in his life when he'd turned to the Lord and had received a solution—not always right away, and the lack of immediacy had molded him into the patient man he was today.

Suddenly a low growl came from Shep.

His dog's ears perked, and his attention was focused on the area behind them.

"Lie down, Shep." Luke dragged Megan to the ground.

He could no longer see the two men on the path, but someone or something was behind them. He lifted his head to scan the woods.

Crack!

A bullet grazed his cheek, a stab of pain radiating outward.

"Someone's behind us. The third guy?" Her eyes wide, Megan reached for her backpack nearby, opened it and pulled out a shirt. She pressed it against his face to stem the blood.

"He must have come down the mountain the way we did."

He took the cloth and held it in place while he surveyed the ditch. "If we move to the other side, the guys on the mountain will have a shot at us, but if we stay here, the other one will close the space between him and us, and we won't know it. I need you to low crawl to that tree stump. Stay behind it."

"Where are you and Shep going to hide?"

He pointed about ten feet away. "We're going to that tall grass."

"You don't have any cover."

"You're the only one who fits behind the trunk. Fire the rifle without exposing yourself. When the guy comes after you, I can take him out. We need to take care of him or the two on the mountain will close in on us."

"Okay." She started crawling away.

"Stay down even lower," Luke warned. "Like soldiers do. Watch me."

With Shep next to him, he began moving in the opposite direction using his elbows and arms on the ground to pull himself forward while his legs pushed him onward. Halfway to the tall, thick grass, he glanced back. Megan reached the large tree stump and scrambled behind it. His dog let out another growl. He suspected the third guy was moving toward the ditch. Luke increased his speed. Reaching his shelter, he quickly pivoted his body, so he could keep an eye on the woods.

As he positioned his gun in order to use it, Sheriff Clinton zigzagged his way from one tree to another until he was only yards away from the edge of the ditch, not far from Megan's location. For a few seconds, Luke wondered if the sheriff had arrived to support them and possibly had taken out the third guy.

Then why didn't Clinton call out to them? Was he the man who was behind what occurred at the school?

Unaware of what was happening, Megan did as he said and poked the barrel of the rifle out and shot it in the direction of the forest without exposing herself. The sheriff didn't return fire, but he raced to the nearest big oak, off to the right and closer to Luke.

Still not a word from the law enforcement officer. He remembered seeing him at the fire that destroyed his house. Had Clinton followed him to the broodmare barn? Had he somehow figured out where Luke was going with Megan? He was trying to remember what they talked about while there. They'd discussed their escape from the farm.

Megan shot again.

Sheriff Clinton rushed toward her, shooting off his weapon several times, bark on the trunk flying in different directions.

Luke raised up enough to get a good shot off. His bullet struck the sheriff in the thigh, sending him stumbling to the ground.

When he started to lift his handgun, Megan leaned to the side and moved out from behind the stump with the rifle pointed at the sheriff. "I'll shoot if you try anything. Push the gun away."

"The same for me," Luke shouted as the sound of vehicles racing toward them filled the air.

For a few seconds the sheriff hesitated then shoved his weapon closer to Megan.

As much as Luke wanted to go to her, he knew he couldn't stand and reveal his location to the two still on the mountain. He did get close to the side of the ditch, so he wasn't a target.

Within minutes, Clay and other police officers showed up. Clay parked his car by the ditch in such a way that Luke and Megan would have cover. "How are you two?"

Megan kept her rifle aimed at the sheriff. "Okay now."

"We can outlast you!" one of the state police near the bottom of the trail shouted to the two still left on the mountain. "We can bring in more officers and keep you pinned down until you die from dehydration. Not a pleasant way to go. Throw out your weapons and put your arms up. Then you slowly move to the trail where we can see both of you."

With the car giving Luke more protection, he made it to the side and low ran to Megan, keeping his gaze trained on Clinton in case he decided to go for his gun, lying between him and her. When he reached her, Luke used a stick to draw the sheriff's weapon to him. "Thanks, Clay, for showing up."

"Part of my job description," Clay said over the round of gunfire exchanged between the other state police and the two assailants. "You two can relax. I've got

Sheriff Clinton in my sights. What happened here?"

Megan put the rifle across her lap and sank back against the dirt wall that had shielded them from the two guys on the mountain who wanted them dead. "The sheriff was with the guys who've been after me. He shot first. We returned fire."

"I've called for an ambulance. We'll sort this out once the others are apprehended."

Over the course of his time in search and rescue, Luke had learned a lot. He might have shot Sheriff Clinton, but he didn't want the man to die. "As soon as your cohorts surrender, I can take a look at your wound. I've been trained in first aid. Use your shirt to stop your bleeding." From the amount of blood from the wound, it didn't appear that he'd hit an artery. For that Luke thanked the Lord.

"It's over," Sheriff Clinton yelled, sweat running down his pain-etched face.

Luke sat next to Megan with Shep on the other side. He took her hand. "All I want is a cold shower, a four-course meal, and a bed."

"Where? Both of our homes are burned down."

"Good question. I'll think of something."

* * *

Hours later, Megan sat in an interview with Chief Franklin and Clay at the police office in Sweetwater City. She'd showered, changed into newly-bought clothes, and ate enough for two meals. Her earlier adrenaline surge had abated, leaving her exhausted both physically and mentally.

Clay gave Megan her mother's ring. "This is yours."

She smiled. "Thanks. I'm so glad it wasn't lost."

"Megan, we've processed the restroom at the elementary school." Chief Franklin set his elbows on the table and clasped his hands together. "The body in your house was Shelly, and now we know where she was murdered. Drummond was killed with a gun found in Sheriff Clinton's house. Are you sure it was Drummond leaving Shelly's crime scene?"

"Yes. The memories came back at first in bits and pieces, but it was him." As she'd showered, the rest of what went down returned to her, leaving her shaken to her core. The fear that had previously swamped her did so again. Her hands began to tremble. She curled them into fists.

"What else?" Clay asked in an encouraging voice.

"Drummond was the one who took me, left me with the two guys in a house. All I saw of it was a bedroom. I was tied to the bed and left in the dark until the thin one came in and gave me a shot. I passed out again. I came to in the trunk of a car with chains tied around my body, lying on plastic bags of drugs. The other one opened it and dragged me out. Then with the help of the thin man, he tossed me off the bridge into the river."

"Do you know why they killed Shelly?"

"Not sure. When Keith Drummond walked away from the restroom, he was carrying something in his hand. Possibly a notebook. I don't know if that had anything to do with it or not." The tension from holding a tight fist snaked up her arms. She had to relax. It was over. She needed to start healing. "After falling into the river, the next thing I remember is Luke reviving me on the bank."

"Ah, that explains a notebook we discovered at the sheriff's house full of names of people with amounts next to them." Clay showed her a photo of it.

"It looks like the right size. It was hard to tell."

Chief Franklin rubbed his jaw. "Why didn't you want to report what happened to me?"

Megan stared into Chief Franklin's kind eyes. "All I could remember was the bad guy was wearing a police uniform. I didn't know what was going on or why. I thought about talking to you, but when my house was destroyed with a body inside, I became even more frightened, especially because I couldn't remember anything about the past twenty-four hours. So, you think all of this concerns a drug ring?"

Chief Franklin glanced at Clay.

The state police officer sat forward.

"Yes. It looks like Shelly was involved as well as Keith Drummond. The two men who tried to kill you confessed that Sheriff Clinton is the head of it. They've made a deal in exchange for information. The state police are rounding up the rest of the ring."

"Involving the students at school?"

"Yes. That most likely was Drummond and Shelly's part."

Megan shifted her attention to the police chief. "How did they find us at the cabin?"

"Sheriff Clinton was at the fire. He followed you to the barn and overheard part of your conversation. He put a tracker on the truck you were taking. According to the big guy that tossed you over the bridge, the sheriff wanted to get rid of you and Luke, but he didn't want your bodies found. That's why they came after you at the cabin."

Megan drew in a deep, calming breath and flexed her hands. What she went through the past several days was worth it if a group of drug traffickers were put out of business. "Do you need anything else from me?"

"Not at the moment. Get some rest. You're safe." Clay closed his folder.

Megan rose. "Chief Franklin, I'm sorry I didn't come to you when it happened."

The police chief stood. "Frankly, I'm not sure we would have discovered everything that was going on under our noses if you had. You've done me a favor." He shook Megan's hand. "Now, I think Luke is waiting for you."

"You're finished talking with him?"

Chief Franklin nodded.

Clay got to his feet and opened the door for Megan. Luke leaned against the wall right outside the interview room. The sight of him sent her heartbeat racing. He straightened and took a step toward her. When he placed his arms around her and hugged her, she felt as though she'd come home. She wouldn't be alive today if he hadn't saved her. But her feelings for him went beyond that.

Smiling, she pulled back to look into his face. "I'm glad a doctor examined the wound on your cheek."

One corner of his mouth tilted up. "I'm going to live but most likely will have a scar. Ready to leave?"

"I'm not sure where I should go."

"I've got a suggestion. Riverdale Farm. There's enough room for you to stay with Liliana and Nadine in the guesthouse. I know it's forty-five minutes from here, but it'll give you some time to figure out what you want to do."

"Rebuild or buy a new home?"

"Those are two options, but there's a third one. I want to get to know you better and see where things go." He cocked a grin. "However, I must admit I already know you pretty well. That's what running for your life can do."

"We'll be like two normal people who've met and started dating?"

He nodded.

"I like the sound of that, especially the normal part. What's been happening certainly isn't normal." Still in his embrace, she closed the space between them until their lips touched each other, and she surrendered to the delicious sensation he generated in her.

EPILOGUE

Valentine's Day the following year

Blindfolded, Megan sat beside Luke as he flew his helicopter. "Where are you taking me?"

Luke chuckled. "Be patient. We're almost there."

Megan relaxed. She was in very capable hands. It probably wasn't a good idea for her to see what was going on since the helicopter would give her a clear view of the ground far below. She'd come a long way in overcoming her fear of heights, but she hadn't quite gotten over it enough to sit calmly as they flew over the landscape without her blindfold on.

They had grown close in the months they'd been together. She'd discovered driving forty-five minutes back and forth to school had been a good thing. It was her quiet time. She had her burned home torn completely down, but she still hadn't come to a decision about what to do with the property. Whereas, Luke's house was almost completely restored. She'd enjoyed helping him and Liliana with decisions concerning their home.

The helicopter began its descent. When it landed, she started to take off the blindfold.

Luke touched her arm. "No, not yet. I'm coming around, and I'll help you out of the helicopter."

"Okay." What was he up to? And why did he bring Shep on this day trip? He was behind her in his kennel.

Luke opened the door on her side and took her hand. With his assistance, she climbed down, a light cool breeze blowing. He hooked his arm through hers and moved forward a few yards.

"You can take off the blindfold now."

When Megan did, she couldn't believe what was before her. She was at the cabin where they'd hidden last August, but it wasn't really the same place. It was bigger and made of logs. A chimney was on one side and there were more windows. A porch along the front had been added. "What happened?"

"I bought the place from my friend and made some changes that will make you feel at home. But that doesn't mean I won't try to get you to rough it in a tent from time to time. Wait here. Let me get Shep. I brought him, so he could be our alarm if a bear comes around although all the times I've been here overseeing its construction I haven't seen that monster." Luke hurried to the helicopter and released Shep from the kennel.

After he returned with Shep by his side, she walked with them to the new cabin. "When did you come here?"

"When you were at school. I wanted this to be a surprise, but it isn't my only one. Let's go inside."

As she stepped into the cabin, shock set in, and she came to a stop. Her jaw dropped as she scanned the main room with new beautiful, rustic furniture that fit the environment. The dominant colors were dark brown with splashes of forest green in the pillows on the couch and the two loungers. The place shouted cozy and homey. Off to the side was a table with four chairs and a kitchen with a small refrigerator and stove as well as a sink.

Megan pointed to the two doors at the back of the cabin. "What's in there?"

"A bathroom with a shower and a bedroom with a super comfortable bed."

She turned to him, stunned that he'd done all of this. "Why?"

He stuck his hand into his leather jacket pocket and withdrew a small box.

When he went down on one knee and took her left hand, Megan brought her other one to her mouth. Everyday she'd been with him, she'd fallen more and more in love with Luke. He was everything she'd dreamed of.

"Megan Witherspoon, I love you. Will

you marry me?"

Words clogged her throat, all her feelings for Luke swamping her. She knelt in front of him. "I love you." She put her arms around him and leaned forward. She brushed her mouth over his then kissed him with all her love in it. When she finally pulled back, she said, "Yes," and held up her left hand for him to slip on her engagement ring.

He embraced her and lowered his head toward hers.

Shep barked.

Startled, Megan drew back. "A bear? Now."

Shep walked over to them and laid his head on Luke's arm hugging Megan.

He laughed. "That's Shep's stamp of approval. Now all we need to get is Lady's."

Megan laughed. "I have a feeling we already have that. She follows you around everywhere."

Dear Reader,

After writing a ten-book series about strong women in extraordinary situations, I'm excited to start a new series called Everyday Heroes. There are so many people in our world that are heroic. I want to showcase stories about ordinary men doing extraordinary deeds. When someone is in trouble, they step up and help, even putting themselves in danger.

I would love your input into what you think is an everyday hero. You can contact me at margaretdaley@gmail.com. Thanks for reading Hunted. I hope you'll leave a review of the book at the retailer where you bought it. For more information about me and my other books, you can visit my website at: www.margaretdaley.com.

Take care,
Margaret Daley

DEADLY HUNT

Book One in
Strong Women, Extraordinary Situations
by Margaret Daley

All bodyguard Tess Miller wants is a vacation. But when a wounded stranger stumbles into her isolated cabin in the Arizona mountains, Tess becomes his lifeline. When Shane Burkhart opens his eyes, all he can focus on is his guardian angel leaning over him. And in the days to come he will need a guardian angel while being hunted by someone who wants him dead.

DEADLY INTENT

Book Two in
Strong Women, Extraordinary Situations
by Margaret Daley

Texas Ranger Sarah Osborn thought she would never see her high school sweetheart, Ian O'Leary, again. But fifteen years later, Ian, an ex-FBI agent, has someone targeting him, and she's assigned to the case. Can Sarah protect Ian and her heart?

DEADLY HOLIDAY

Book Three in
Strong Women, Extraordinary Situations
by Margaret Daley

Tory Caldwell witnesses a hit-and-run, but when the dead victim disappears from the scene, police doubt a crime has been committed. Tory is threatened when she keeps insisting she saw a man killed and the only one who believes her is her neighbor, Jordan Steele. Together, can they solve the mystery of the disappearing body and stay alive?

DEADLY COUNTDOWN

Book Four in
Strong Women, Extraordinary Situations
by Margaret Daley

Allie Martin, a widow, has a secret protector who manipulates her life without anyone knowing until...

When Remy Broussard, an injured police officer, returns to Port David, Louisiana to visit before his medical leave is over, he discovers his childhood friend, Allie Martin, is being stalked. As Remy protects Allie and tries to find her stalker, they realize their feelings go beyond friendship.

When the stalker is found, they begin to explore the deeper feelings they have for each other, only to have a more sinister threat come between them. Will Allie be able to save Remy before he dies at the hand of a maniac?

DEADLY NOEL

Book Five in
Strong Women, Extraordinary Situations
by Margaret Daley

Assistant DA, Kira Davis, convicted the wrong man—Gabriel Michaels, a single dad with a young daughter. When new evidence was brought forth, his conviction was overturned, and Gabriel returned home to his ranch to put his life back together. Although Gabriel is free, the murderer of his wife is still out there and resumes killing women. In a desperate alliance, Kira and Gabriel join forces to find the true identity of the person terrorizing their town. Will they be able to forgive the past and find the killer before it's too late?

DEADLY LEGACY

Book Seven in
Strong Women, Extraordinary Situations
by Margaret Daley

Legacy of Secrets. Threats and Danger. Second Chances.

Down on her luck, single mom, Lacey St. John, believes her life has finally changed for the better when she receives an inheritance from a wealthy stranger. Her ancestral home she'd thought forever lost has been transformed into a lucrative bed and breakfast guaranteed to bring much-needed financial security. Her happiness is complete until strange happenings erode her sense of well being. When her life is threatened, she turns to neighbor and police detective, Ryan McNeil, for help. He promises to solve the mystery of who's ruining her newfound peace of mind, but when her troubles escalate to the point that her every move leads to danger, she's unsure who to trust. Is the strong, capable neighbor she's falling for as amazing as he seems? Or could he be the man who wants her dead?

DEADLY NIGHT, SILENT NIGHT

Book Eight in
Strong Women, Extraordinary Situations
by Margaret Daley

Revenge. Sabotage. Second Chances.

Widow Rebecca Howard runs a successful store chain that is being targeted during the holiday season. Detective Alex Kincaid, best friends with Rebecca's twin brother, is investigating the hacking of the store's computer system. When the attacks become personal, Alex must find the assailant before Rebecca, the woman he's falling in love with, is murdered.

DEADLY FIRES

Book Nine in
Strong Women, Extraordinary Situations
by Margaret Daley

Second Chances. Revenge. Arson.

A saboteur targets Alexia Richards and her family company. As the incidents become more lethal, Alexia must depend on a former Delta Force soldier, Cole Knight, a man from her past that she loved. When their son died in a fire, their grief and anger drove them apart. Can Alexia and Cole work through their pain and join forces to find the person who wants her dead?

DEADLY SECRETS

Book Ten in
Strong Women, Extraordinary Situations
by Margaret Daley

Secrets. Murder. Reunion.

Sarah St. John, an FBI profiler, finally returns home after fifteen years for her niece's wedding. But in less than a day, Sarah's world is shattered when her niece is kidnapped the night before her vows. Sarah can't shake the feeling her own highly personal reason for leaving Hunter Davis at the altar is now playing out again in this nightmarish scene with her niece.

Sarah has to work with Detective Hunter Davis, her ex-fiancé, to find her niece before the young woman becomes the latest victim of a serial killer. Sarah must relive part of her past in order to assure there is a future for her niece and herself. Can Sarah and Hunter overcome their painful past and work together before the killer strikes again?

About the Author

Margaret Daley, a USA Today's Bestselling author of over 105 books (five million plus sold worldwide), has been married for over forty-seven years and is a firm believer in romance and love. When she isn't traveling or being with her two granddaughters, she's writing love stories, often with a suspense/mystery thread and corralling her cats that think they rule her household. To find out more about Margaret visit her website at www.margaretdaley.com.

Facebook:
www.facebook.com/margaretdaleybooks

Twitter:
twitter.com/margaretdaley

Link to sign up for my newsletter on front page of website: www.margaretdaley.com

Made in the USA
Coppell, TX
11 April 2021